Almost the Right Girl

Ellie Khelliver

Published by Ellie Khelliver, 2023.

ALMOST THE RIGHT GIRL

First edition. June 10, 2023.

ISBN: 979-8223978572

Written by Ellie Khelliver.

Table of Contents

Chapter 1

September Ellis switched her backpack to her other shoulder and shifted her weight. She'd been standing in line to talk to someone in housing for almost an hour. She was finally at the front of the line, and just in time too. If she had to listen to any more talk from the two idiotic frat boys behind her about nailing new sorority pledges at their next party while 'accidentally' brushing up against her ass one more time, she was going to slug somebody. This day had to get better soon. It certainly couldn't get much worse. September's shoulder twinged and reminded her how much worse it could be. She shook her head and took a deep breath to hold off the unwanted memories. If she thought about Lizzie now, she'd cry.

"Next please!" The blond, haggard looking woman in the black suit put the papers in front of her into a gray metal tray on the side of her work-piled desk. September left the touchy-feely frat boys behind, sat down in the wooden chair across from the woman, and reached into her black leather backpack. The woman's watery blue eyes were lifeless behind the wire frames of her glasses. "Can I help you?"

"I applied for a dorm room-."

"Residence hall." The woman automatically corrected her. The woman's swivel chair squeaked as she leaned towards September, her eyes focusing on something behind September.

"Whatever. I sent you my application and deposit and you sent me this letter." September handed a slightly crumpled letter on official Eastern New Mexico University stationery to the woman. "That letter says that I am supposed to be in room 230 in DeBaca Hall. When I got here today and tried to check in, they told me they had no record of me, and the room was full!"

The woman reluctantly took the letter from her and looked at it. "There's obviously been some kind of mistake-."

"Yes! You cashed my check and sent me a letter telling me I had a room! The resident adviser over there told me there aren't any more rooms on campus. Just because I'm not rushing a sorority and wasn't here a week earlier for rush doesn't mean those two girls who showed up at the last minute should get to keep my room!"

"Let me check the computer and see if I can find something." The woman typed some things into her computer while September stared at the generic inspirational posters decorating the office walls. There must be some sort of law dictating what school officials were allowed to decorate their offices with. The school offices at the University of Oklahoma looked exactly the same.

The woman finally turned back to September. She took off her glasses and rubbed her forehead before speaking. "I'm sorry. I can't find any open rooms on campus. Since the other girls were here first, we have to let them keep the room. It's school policy."

"But that's not fair!"

September couldn't believe it. She'd gotten up at the butt crack of dawn, driven eight hours from Oklahoma City to find no room ready, and now this woman was telling her they couldn't help her even though it was their fault! This was absolutely ridiculous. She'd put up with having her ass grabbed for an hour for this?

"We can put you at the top of our waiting list. There are always some people who don't show up for school. We have to hold their rooms for two weeks, but then we can give them to the students on the waiting list. That's the best we can do."

September stood up. "Two weeks? What am I supposed to do in the meantime? It's not my fault you all screwed up!"

"That's all we can do. I am sorry." The woman started shifting papers around on her desk, dismissing September without looking at her.

"No. I want my deposit back. I'm not waiting two weeks for the possibility of a room. I'll find something off campus." September grabbed her backpack from the floor and slung it over her shoulder. They'd better think twice if they thought they were keeping her deposit.

She quickly pushed aside the thoughts that she hadn't seen anything even remotely resembling an apartment building during the short drive through town, and she didn't want to live alone. Having her own room in a dorm was one thing, living completely alone was another.

"It will take two days to process your refund. I need your signature on this form." The woman opened a desk drawer and slid a piece of paper across the desk.

"Fine." September impatiently shoved a piece of long red hair behind her ear and hurriedly signed her name on the paper the woman handed her. She let the door slam behind her as she left the housing office.

She stepped outside the Student Union, bought a Diet Pepsi from the soda machine, and went inside. At OU, the student union had a bulletin board where people could hang up ads, and she was sure it would be the same here. She quickly managed to find the community bulletin board on a wall in the stairwell between floors. She got out a spiral notebook and pen and began to search the ads.

September scanned the board. Car for Sale, Textbooks for Sale, Swing Dance Lessons, Lose Weight Now for a Brand New You in 1993. No, no, no. Finally, she found the Roommates Wanted ads. Let's see... Couple Seeks Third, dream on. Single Guy Seeks Pretty Female Roommate, definitely not! Walking Distance to Campus, that could be good. September wrote down the information for that ad and moved on to the next one. $625 a month rent, they've got to be kidding, skip that one. Girl with Dog Seeks Nonsmoking Roommate, maybe, although I'm not crazy about the idea of dog hair all over everything.

When September had eliminated all the obvious potential freaks and weirdos, and had finished looking at the board, she had found five possible roommate situations. She decided to get a map at the Student Union information center and take it to the fountain in the center of campus to get organized and decide where to call the ads. She needed a place to sleep tonight, but she doubted the hotel in town would be full. If it was full by some miracle, the town, Clovis, that she'd driven through on her way to Portales, looked like it had a few more hotels.

This is too hard. The thought hit September suddenly and without warning. Panic spread through her chest. *This isn't as good of an idea as I thought.* If I get into my car now, I can be home by midnight. I could stay with Spring and get re-enrolled at OU. September took a few steps in the direction of her car and stopped. She took a deep breath, counted to four, and let it out slowly. She repeated the process several times until the panic started to recede. *No! I am not running.* Dr. Clark and I talked about this, and it is a good idea for me to be here. Things were hard at home too. I can do this.

Taking one more deep breath, September took a big drink of her soda and released some more of her tension. She took the time to really look around her for the first time.

The campus was small, but pretty. The red brick buildings were arranged in an oval with sidewalks that conjoined around the fountain in the center of campus. The sidewalks were wet in places where the sprinklers were watering more sidewalk than grass. September could see both ends of campus from where she stood. Despite the seeming lack of grass and trees in town, the campus was green and had lots of shade trees everywhere.

As September approached the fountain, she saw a dark-haired girl in denim cutoffs and an olive-green tank top lying on one of the eight benches surrounding the fountain. The girl's legs were tan and smooth. Her toenails peeking out from a pair of Birkenstocks had flecks of blue polish on them from a long-forgotten pedicure. Her cropped tank top hugged her curves and ended just above her belted shorts. Her sunglasses made September wish once more that she hadn't left her sunglasses in her car. The girl was wearing headphones and didn't seem to be paying much attention to the book she had propped up on her thighs. There was a drink and a lumpy looking plaid flannel lying on the brick walk beside her. September wasn't sure, but she thought the girl was watching her as she sat down on one of the wooden benches.

"Those campus maps are heinous. You'll never find anything. Besides, this is pretty much it." The girl closed her book and set it on the bench beside her as she sat up.

September looked towards the girl with the dark, curly hair and olive skin who had spoken to her. She looked familiar for some reason. "Thanks. It's a town map. I'm trying to figure out what would be considered close to campus."

Eyes still hidden by her sunglasses, the girl seemed to look September up and down, taking in her white t-shirt and short black sundress, before speaking again. "Want some help?"

"That'd be great. Thanks." September brought the map and set it in front of the girl who leaned over and started pointing at a section in the corner. *At least one person on this campus is friendly.*

"Here's campus. This is the highway. Avenue J is close. There are usually tons of houses for rent on these two streets. Stay away from Main though. It floods like crazy when it rains. Rent's pretty cheap. You could-."

Without warning, she stopped talking and reached under the flannel shirt on the ground. She pulled out a neon green and orange super soaker water gun and jumped to her feet, pointing at something behind September. Warily, September got to her feet too and turned to see a dark-haired guy in a white Sigma Nu t-shirt and baggy tan shorts pointing a similar gun at her.

"What's going on?" September stood between them, eying them both uneasily. This place was getting stranger by the minute.

"Move if you don't want to get wet." The girl warned without taking her eyes off the guy as she spoke to September.

"Get lost, Red. This doesn't concern you." The guy quickly glanced in her direction and then back as he took a step closer.

"Take one more step and kiss your ass goodbye, Brian." The girl pumped her neon-colored water gun, so it was ready to shoot.

September stood between them, watching the face off. Brian glanced at her and back to the girl. "I said move it, Red." He reached out, grabbed her arm roughly, and shoved her out of the way.

September jerked backwards, her fight or flight response momentarily flared as she fought to keep from running away. She took a deep breath. That was it. Anger overtook fear. She'd had it with frat boys today. This idiot was not getting away with shoving her.

Rubbing her arm, she walked over to her belongings on the bench behind Brian and picked up her warm soda can. September calmly poured the rest of it over his head. Furious, he lowered his gun and spun around to confront her. As he reached for her, the girl dropped to her knees and fired.

"You bitch! Why'd you-?" A stream of cold water hit Brian on the back of his head. He spun back around. But it was too late. "Hey! That's not fair! Your friend distracted me. That doesn't count." He threw his water gun down in protest.

The girl stood up and shrugged. "I just met her. I don't even know her name. I got you fair and square. You're dead. My team wins." The girl raised her gun over her head and did a small victory dance. September smiled.

"No way!" Brian shook his head angrily.

"You shouldn't have shoved me." September threw her empty soda can into the recycling bin beside the bench and sat down again by the map. The girl sat back down, laughing as she watched Brian storm off, covered in soda.

September joined in as she shifted positions to avoid the puddle of soda that had formed on the ground by where Brian had been standing. "Is he a friend of yours?"

"Not really. He's the boy toy of a girl who plays, so by association he gets to play too."

"So, you chase each other around with water guns?"

"Pretty much, yeah. We have rules, like you can't stake out someone's house or class, if you both shoot at the same time you're both dead, things like that. It's wild. This is the last game before school starts."

September looked up as the sky suddenly went dark. The sky that had been blue and cloudless a few moments ago was filled with dark clouds. "What the-?"

The girl looked up and smiled as she felt a drop of rain hit her face. "Grab your stuff!"

"What? Why?"

"Cuz it's about to pour!" The girl was stuffing her Walkman and book into her flannel. She gathered it up into a bundle and held it to her chest. September quickly gathered up her things as she felt raindrops begin to fall. Right as she shoved the last of her belongings into her backpack, the sky opened up and rain began pouring down in sheets, making the sidewalk as slippery as glass. The girl grabbed her hand. "Follow me!"

Chapter 2

"Bathroom's in there. The towel on the rack is clean. I'll lend you some clothes and I can put your dress in the dryer." She pointed September to a white painted door in the middle of a short hallway and disappeared into a room at the end of the hall. September stepped into the small but neat bathroom and gingerly pulled the large black towel off the metal towel rack. She stood on the black bathmat, leaned over the white cracked tub and started towel drying her hair as she looked at the black and white swirled shower curtain and white porcelain sink. The tub, toilet, and sink were clean, but had the not quite white look of old fixtures. A Sailor Moon sticker was stuck to the lower right-hand corner of the mirror. The girl's arm appeared in the doorway, a blue shirt and denim cutoffs in hand. "Here. Come into the living room when you're done."

"Thanks." September took the clothes and set them on the counter.

September closed the door as the girl's arm disappeared from the doorway. The back of the door had a hook that held a long, red, terry cloth robe that September thought looked really comfortable. At the moment, all she wanted to do was take a long, hot bubble bath, and then wrap herself in a soft robe and read a book. She was worn out and she still had to find a place to live.

September stripped off her soggy dress and t-shirt and began toweling herself dry. The door opened without warning and a tall, muscular blond guy in a Porn Star t-shirt carrying a box full of towels and toiletries walked in and stopped at the sight of September in her underwear.

"Hey!" She hurriedly wrapped the towel around her, very aware of his gaze lingering on her breasts before traveling down her legs.

"Sorry. I didn't know Mattie was home." His gaze was anchored somewhere between her chest and her face.

"Do you mind?" September pulled the towel tighter around her, thankful it was big enough to almost reach her knees. She shifted her hair, so it fell over her right shoulder, covering her scar.

"What's the big deal? If Mattie's going to photograph you people are going to see more than your underwear." He seemed completely unfazed to find a strange, half-naked woman in his bathroom. September stared at him for a moment, trying to process what he was babbling about.

"What the hell are you talking about? Get out and let me get dressed!" He was way too comfortable with the situation for her taste. She tried to shove him out the door and keep a firm grip on the towel at the same time. The girl appeared in the doorway; her dry flannel shirt half unbuttoned. She rolled her eyes when she saw the blond guy in the bathroom.

September's mouth went dry, and her heart felt like it was going to explode out of her chest. Without her sunglasses, the girl was the spitting image of Lizzie. She had come to New Mexico to escape Lizzie. She closed her eyes and opened them again, hoping the girl would magically look different when she opened them. Nope, still Lizzie's twin. She tried to breathe slowly to calm herself.

"Vincent! Get out!"

Vincent suddenly looked nervous. "Mattie, I thought you'd be at Kate's or something."

"Well, I'm not. You're majorly invading this girl's privacy. Now get out, you idiot." Mattie shoved him out of the bathroom and shut the door behind her. September grabbed the clothes off the counter and dressed quickly. She opened the bathroom door and stepped out into the hallway where Mattie and Vincent were still standing, staring at each other.

Mattie gestured to the box Vincent was holding, her eyes narrowed suspiciously. "What's that?"

"Umm, some of my stuff." Vincent looked towards the hallway and then quickly back at Mattie. She pushed past September, walked into the room at the end of the hall, and then reappeared in the doorway.

"You wanna share something with me, Vincent? Your room is almost empty."

September looked at the two of them and cautiously moved out of what she believed to be the line of fire. She didn't even know these people; she didn't want to get in the middle of a lover's quarrel. She had enough problems of her own to deal with. Mattie stood with her arms crossed over her chest. Even though she was a good five inches shorter than Vincent, somehow September had no doubt she was the more dangerous of the two.

"Sorry, Mattie. I was hoping to get out of here before you got home. When I was visiting my parents, I met a girl. She wants me to move in with her." Vincent shrugged.

"You met a girl? You met a girl while you were home and now, two weeks later, you're moving back to Ohio, and you weren't even going to tell me?" Mattie's voice got higher and higher.

September sighed to herself as she sat down on the couch. This was definitely not good. This day was getting worse.

"I was gonna leave you a note." Vincent set the box down on the floor.

"Leave me a note? You were going to leave me a note? How can you do this to me? Rent's due in three days, Vincent!"

"Sorry. Patty's cute, and I'm tired of this town. I got fired yesterday, so I figured why not?" Vincent seemed completely unfazed by her anger. September had trouble picturing the two of them together.

Mattie let out a yell of frustration. "You owe me, Vincent. You can't move out with no warning right before rent's due."

"I need the money for my trip. Sorry, Mattie." Vincent walked past her into the bathroom and began throwing things into his box. Mattie followed him. September stayed where she was. She wanted to be as far away as possible.

Vincent pushed past Mattie and went over to the stereo in the living room and started pulling cassettes and CDs out of the racks and throwing them into the box. Mattie pulled two of them back out and put them on the scarred coffee table. "Those are mine."

Vincent grabbed them back. "No, they're mine."

September was still sitting on the couch, watching the scene in amazement. When Mattie grabbed a mug off the coffee table and hurled it at Vincent, September dropped to the floor. She watched the two of them throw things at each other and yell as she tried to crawl towards her backpack.

Rain or no rain, in someone else's clothes or not, she was not going to stay in this house another minute. She grabbed her backpack, and it caught on a nail sticking out of the doorframe, ripping the handle and spilling her things onto the floor.

"Shit!" Mattie and Vincent stopped fighting and turned to stare at her as she sank to her knees on the carpet, picking up pens, makeup, keys, and other items, shoving them back into her pack. She paused when she picked up her notebook, staring at the now unreadable page where her ads had been written down. It was the last straw. She dropped the notebook and the backpack and put her head in her hands, slumping against the wall.

Vincent shifted uncomfortably as September began to cry in frustration. Mattie glanced at him, and sighing, motioned towards the door. Vincent grabbed his box and headed out the door, mumbling another apology to Mattie. Mattie sat down on the carpet beside September and put a hand on her shoulder.

"Are you okay?" Her voice held none of the threatening quality it had while yelling at Vincent. If she hadn't just seen the fight with her own eyes, September would never have believed this girl was capable of throwing things at someone almost twice her size.

September sniffed and wiped her eyes with the backs of her hands. She hated crying in front of people she didn't know. "Yeah. I'm sorry. It's been a very long, very bad day. The school lost my room reservation and now my ads are gone."

"And you had to endure that scene between me and Vincent. Sorry. It's not usually nearly this insane." Mattie stood up and helped September to her feet. "Let me make you some chamomile tea. When the rain stops, I'll help you with the ads. I owe you."

"Okay." September managed to give Mattie a smile. She couldn't look her in the face, or she might cry again. Mattie went into the kitchen and September eyed the CDs and cassettes. She'd never heard of Ani DiFranco, Sleater Kinney, or Team Dresch and idly looked over the covers before putting them back. Mattie came back into the living room with the tea. September joined her on the couch.

"In case you didn't catch it, I'm Mattie Wilson." The girl handed her a thick blue mug. "It's hot."

"I'm September Ellis."

"That's an interesting name. How'd you get it?" Mattie tucked both her legs underneath her on the sofa as she settled back into the cushions and took a cautious sip of tea.

"My parents were hippies. The month of September was a good one for them so they thought it would be lucky. I have an older sister named Spring."

Mattie was quiet for a moment and then looked at September. She seemed to be wrestling with something. "How much were you planning on paying for rent?"

"I'm not sure, why?"

"You need a place to live and as you saw, I suddenly need a roommate. Rent here is two hundred a month plus half the bills which is usually about seventy-five." She paused. "What do you think?"

"I don't know." September eyed the broken mug in the corner. She wanted a place to live, but she wasn't sure Mattie was someone she wanted to live with. She could obviously be volatile. She also wasn't sure she could handle living with a girl who could be Lizzie's twin.

"I swear I'm not a psycho. I don't throw things a lot, and I really regret throwing that mug. It was my favorite." Mattie smiled. Even her smile looked like Lizzie's.

"I guess I could give it a try." September hoped she wasn't making a big mistake, but the idea of being done with the day and having a place to live had too much pull to be ignored. It had been a horrible day, and Mattie's smile felt like home, even if she was a stranger.

"Great!" Mattie pulled September off the couch, led her down the hall, opened a door and swept her arms in a grand gesture towards the empty room. "Your room, my lady."

"This is great. I can set up my workbench in that corner." The room was perfect. September was already picturing where to put her bookshelf and supplies. Maybe this wouldn't be so bad.

"Workbench?"

"I'm an art student. I mostly do clay sculpture and jewelry." September let her eyes wander over the empty space.

It was a good-sized room with blinds that had seen better days and spots on the walls where the ghost outlines of long-gone objects could be seen. Considering it had carpet, a decent closet, twice the space of a dorm room and only one person to share a bathroom with, September thought she might actually have gotten lucky.

"Wanna see the rest of the pad?"

"Sure." September followed Mattie to the next door in the hall.

"This is my studio. I'm an art student too. I'm a photographer." Mattie opened the door. The windows in this room had been covered with heavy black drapes. Against the far wall was a large piece of white canvas hanging from the ceiling and stretched part way down to the floor. A tripod with a 35 mm camera stood in front of the whole set up. In one of the far corners was a pile of various props on top of a mattress and makeshift bed frame. Beside that was a rack with various clothing hanging from it. Next to the door was a portable stereo and a stack of cassettes and CDs. A small table with lenses and film canisters stood beside it.

The walls without the canvas were covered with photographs. Some were color, and some were black and white. A few of the photos were framed, but most were pinned to the walls with thumbtacks. Mattie was serious about her work. A lot of time and effort had gone into setting up this studio. The rest of the house was neat, but comfortably lived in. The studio was organized to within an inch of its life.

September looked at some of the prints nearest her. Women of various ages filled all of the images. The black and white image of a nude woman's back as she lifted her long, curly hair to expose her neck caught September's attention. The photo next to that was of a nude blond woman in a dance pose behind a net veil, three dimensional butterflies obscuring important anatomical details. Most of the photos were sensual in nature and September began to understand Vincent's odd comments earlier. There were a few photos of a young girl with a puppy in the grass and some photos of Mattie standing in a dense wooded area, partially hidden by foliage.

"These are beautiful." September moved closer so she could study the photos more carefully. Her new roommate was incredibly good.

"Thanks. Maybe you'll pose for me some time." Most of Mattie's models were friends of hers or people she saw on the street and asked to pose for her. She almost always had a camera with her.

Mattie had wanted to photograph September from the moment she'd seen her walking across campus. Her pale skin was unmarked by the freckles that often accompanied red hair. Her deep, fire-red hair hung almost to her waist and her large green eyes would leap out of the photos. What made Mattie want to photograph her most of all was the slight sadness September seemed to have.

"Maybe. I'm not sure I'm model material." September ducked past Mattie into the hall. She knew Mattie would see the scar on her shoulder at some point, but she was self-conscious and hadn't figured out how she wanted to explain it yet.

"You'd be incredible. I have great visions of the images I could create with that hair of yours." Mattie closed the door behind her. "If there's a piece of paper hanging on the door, it means I'm working and don't want to be disturbed."

"Okay." September followed Mattie to the end of the hall.

"You've seen the bathroom. We share that. This is my room. It's got a bathroom attached, but I turned it into a darkroom."

September looked through Mattie's open door and saw an unmade double bed with black sheets on it and a hardwood floor, which was partially covered by a worn rag rug. The walls were hung with poster prints of famous art combined with framed prints September guessed were Mattie's.

September followed Mattie back to the living room and looked around more closely. There was a large bookcase near the front door mostly filled with books, but with a couple of shelves still free. The couch wasn't actually velour, but rather draped with a red velour blanket. There was a floor lamp next to the couch and an off-white chair at a right angle to the coffee table. A television and VCR with a few video tapes stacked on top stood in the corner across from the couch. More of Mattie's prints were hanging on the walls. The floor was covered in the same beige carpet that was in her room, the studio, and the hall. There was a space in the corner that would be perfect for displaying one of her sculptures.

She looked out the living room window and saw that the rain had stopped. "I guess I can go get my car and start moving my things in."

"I'll pull the mattress in my studio into your room. You can use it until you get a bed."

"Thanks, Liz-Mattie." September grabbed her keys and then paused. "Can you tell me how to get back to DeBaca Hall?"

Chapter 3

September had gotten through her first two weeks of classes with only one anxiety attack, and she'd only caught herself calling Mattie by Lizzie's name twice. She was declaring the week a success and was thinking about going to the local video store to rent a movie to celebrate when someone knocked on the door.

"Oh my God! Spring, what're you doing here?" September pulled her older sister into a hug as she stepped inside. She looked over her sister's shoulder and frowned when she saw the small U-Haul trailer attached to Spring's car. "Are Mom and Dad with you? Are you moving in?"

Spring laughed. "No. Mom said since you weren't in the dorm, she wanted you to have some of your things from home. I think she really just wanted me to check up on you." Spring pulled out of September's embrace and took a step back so she could study September's face. "How are you doing?"

September pulled out of her sister's grasp and turned her head away from Spring's gaze. She should have expected something like this. Her mother called every day, sometimes twice. September loved her parents. She was close with them and appreciated everything they had done in the past year, but they were smothering her, and she wasn't even in the same state.

She'd already arranged to have her own phone line installed. The frequency with which her parents called was beginning to be embarrassing. Last year was the first time anything remotely tragic had touched their family and they were leaning towards being overprotective.

"I'm okay. Really. I like it here." She slipped past her sister and walked towards the trailer. She knew she wouldn't be able to avoid the conversation completely, but she didn't want to have it right at this moment. "What did Mom send?"

"Groceries of course. She sent tons of those disgusting Snoball things you love. She also sent one of your dressers and a bookcase Dad painted. She packed up another box of your books, some more of your clothes, and one of your bricks of clay. Unfortunately, she also sent that hideous lamp from the living room." Spring opened the back of the trailer.

"I like that lamp! It's so ugly it's cute." September pulled the box that held the lamp out of the trailer and began carrying it into the house. She led the way to her room and set the box on her bed.

"This is new." Spring pointed to the small statue on the workbench that was waiting to be painted.

September shrugged. "It sucks. I still can't get back into the groove. It's a good thing I signed up for a beginning painting class this semester."

"That reminds me." Spring reached into her pocket. "Mom also sent this check."

"Another check? They've got to quit sending me money. I'm fine."

Spring watched her sister's rant with an amused smile. "Are you done? Mom sold two of your necklaces and a statue at the gallery."

"Oh. Cool." September took the check and laughed with her sister. "Let's go for a walk. We can unload the rest later."

"What's that building?" Spring pointed to a large red brick building slightly out of the oval the other buildings formed. September knew Spring was trying to distract her from the fact that she was studying her to see how she was feeling.

"That's the theater. Up there is the fountain where I met Lizzie-I mean Mattie." September pulled a leaf off the tree they were passing and absently rubbed it between her fingers. "If we keep going this way there's a park we can stop at."

"Okay." Spring studied her younger sister with concern. "You sure picked a small town to get lost in."

"Yeah. I didn't expect it to be quite this small. I think I'll like it though." September sat down in a swing. "It's a friendly place." She rocked back and forth, swinging without actually lifting her feet off the ground.

"Mom and Dad are worried about you. I am too." Spring's voice suddenly sounded thick to September. She and Spring had always been close, and September could see the frustration and pain in Spring's eyes at not being able to help her little sister.

"I know." September pushed a piece of long hair behind her ear and stared at the ground for a moment. It looked like the conversation was going to happen now whether she wanted it to or not. "I know you all are worried about me, and I know you love me. This is just something I have to do. I couldn't stand having Mom hover over me all the time anymore."

"Are you–?" Spring broke off the question as September leapt out of the swing, hair swirling around her, and faced her sister. She knew her family was concerned, but she was tired of being watched and questioned all the time. She felt like a bug under a microscope. It was one of the reasons she'd decided to go to New Mexico. It was nice not having someone watch her all the time. She answered this question from her mother every day. She didn't want to have to answer to Spring too.

"Yes, I'm taking my medicine, and yes, I know where to find a counselor at school if I need one!" September started walking, not bothering to look back and see if her sister was coming. She refused to be a bug anymore. Spring hurried to vacate her swing and followed. "Can you please just go back and tell them I'm doing what I'm supposed to? I'm going to be fine, just not overnight!"

"September, I'm sorry. Please don't be mad. I miss having you around. We all do."

"I know. I miss you all too. It's just–I'm hundreds of miles away, and it still feels like they're hovering, you know? Mom calls me every day.

I've only been here two weeks, and Dad has sent money twice already. Now they have you show up on my doorstep without telling me, and–." She sighed as all the fight drained out of her. She shouldn't be mad at them for being concerned. It was a miracle she hadn't died last year.

"You're lucky it was me. I had to talk Mom out of coming herself." Spring tossed an arm around her sister's shoulders.

"Thanks." September gave Spring a brief hug and then opened the door. "Do you want a Diet Pepsi?" September could never stay mad at Spring for long. She really did miss her sister. They could talk about anything.

"That would be great. It's so freaking hot here!"

"Yeah, but they keep telling me at least it's a dry heat."

"What does that even mean?"

"I have no idea." September and Spring laughed as they walked into the living room.

At the sound of voices, Mattie and her friend, Kate, looked up from the photos they had spread on the living room floor. "Oh my God, there are two of her." Kate stared in disbelief at September and her sister in the doorway.

Spring was only an inch shorter than her sister and had the same slender build, high cheekbones and green eyes. Her hair was also long, straight and red, but it was more of a strawberry blond color than the deep red September's was. They were both wearing cut-off shorts and clinging t-shirts. September's was purple and Spring's was green.

"You're not moving out too, are you?" Mattie eyed the girl next to September with interest. Pictures of the two of them together would be incredible. "I can't afford to lose another roommate so quickly."

September laughed. "No. This is my sister, Spring. She brought me some stuff from home. This is my roommate, Mattie, and her friend, Kate."

Spring managed to erase the look of shock from her face and smile as she shook hands with both of them. "I've heard a lot about you,

Mattie." Mattie smiled back and laughed, but Kate's frown that had appeared when September introduced her deepened. She stepped closer to Mattie and put her hand on Mattie's shoulder.

"I'm afraid to ask what. September didn't tell me you were coming. If you two want the living room, we can take these photos into the studio." Mattie began picking up the photographs. She was trying to decide which photos to submit for her first class assignment.

"I didn't know, she surprised me. Don't move. We can go to my room."

"No, it's okay. It might be easier to decide if I hang them up on the walls." Kate picked up some of the pictures and silently followed Mattie out of the room.

Kate closed the door to the studio. "You still haven't told her I'm your girlfriend?"

Mattie sighed, put down the photos she was holding and put her arms around Kate. She ran her hand over the blond's hair and gently kissed her. "I'll tell her. It's just been so crazy with classes starting and her trying to get settled in. As soon as her sister leaves, I swear."

"Maybe her sister will take her home with her."

"Kate, be nice. She's sweet." Mattie sighed. "She's my roommate. You two are going to have to learn to play nice."

"I don't want to fight; I just hate hearing her call me your friend. I'm getting another drink. I'll be right back." Kate left the studio, and paused at the hallway entrance when she heard September and her sister talking.

"Your roommate seems nice. You weren't kidding about her resemblance to Lizzie." Spring paused. The two could almost be twins. "Have you told her? Are you going to tell her? How do you not call her Lizzie all the time?"

"I don't want to tell her, but I think I'm going to have to. She saw me taking my medication the other day. I'm sure she's curious about that and about why you guys call me so often. I've slipped a couple times. I don't think she noticed." September just needed to find the right time. She and Mattie were just getting to know each other. She didn't want Mattie to feel sorry for her or treat her like she was broken.

Kate went back into the studio without getting her drink. Mattie looked at her empty hands, confused. "I think you'd better have that talk soon. Sounds like she's got something to tell you too."

Chapter 4

Mattie knew Kate was right, so she'd asked September if she wanted to hang out and get to know each other better the night after Spring left.

"I didn't think you liked green peppers." September frowned as Mattie pulled a piece of pepper off her pizza and ate it.

"I love them." Mattie wiped her fingers on a napkin and smiled as September shook her head. She still managed to confuse things Lizzie had liked or hated with Mattie. "I'm glad you were home."

"Me too. I haven't seen *House of Yes* in a long time." September took a drink of her soda.

"You've seen it before?" Mattie reached for another piece of veggie pizza on the coffee table in front of them.

"I saw it with a friend when it was in the theater." September twisted the silver ring on her finger and stared down at the carpet. She was trying to work up her nerve to talk to Mattie.

Mattie gestured to the photo album on the coffee table beside the pizza. September had been looking through it when Mattie came home with the movie and pizza. "Do you mind if I look at your pictures?"

"No, go ahead." September stood up and headed for the kitchen. "Do you want another drink?"

"Yeah, thanks." Mattie opened the album and began flipping through the pages. September sat down and handed her the can of Blue Sky. "What was this?" Mattie pointed to a picture of September and a group of girls dressed up in can-can outfits.

September laughed. "That was a play I was in my senior year of high school. It was a blast. We were on stage most of the time, but we didn't actually have any lines. We did a lot of improvisation and drove the director crazy. He never knew what we were going to do next."

Mattie looked through some more pictures with September occasionally pointing out people. "Is this your mom?" Mattie pointed to an attractive green-eyed woman with short red hair the same color as September's.

"Yeah. There's Spring when she was ten, and that's my dad, grandma, and uncle."

A girl with curly dark hair, blue eyes, and a friendly smile was in most of the pictures on the next page. In almost every one of them, she and September had an arm around each other, or arms linked. September had pictures of the girl in her room too. Mattie stared at a picture of the girl in a shirt just like the one she was wearing. September looked at the picture and back at Mattie. "You two look alike, huh?"

Mattie decided it was time to tell September the truth about Kate. "Who is she? She's in a lot of your pictures. You have her picture in your room too. Is she your girlfriend?"

September laughed. "No. Lizzie wasn't my girlfriend. Lots of people thought that though. We were very close." September reached over and closed the book. She knew she had to talk about Lizzie, but she didn't want to. It would be easier now that Mattie had given her an opening. It was now or never.

"I'm sorry. I didn't mean to–I just thought–." Mattie ran her hand through her curls and sat back on the couch. "Look, I probably should have told you this before you moved in, but I didn't."

"Tell me what?" September knew there was something going on. Mattie and Kate were constantly whispering and going into rooms by themselves. She was suddenly afraid Mattie was going to kick her out so Kate could move in.

"Kate's more than a friend." Mattie twisted a curl around her finger.

"What do you mean, more than a friend?" September frowned. She didn't quite get where Mattie was going with this.

"I like girls. Kate's my girlfriend."

"Your girlfriend? I thought you and Vincent were-." September let her sentence trail off. She hadn't even thought about the possibility that Kate was Mattie's girlfriend. She'd been sure Vincent was Mattie's boyfriend. It made more sense than Mattie and Vincent together though.

"I'm sorry I didn't tell you sooner. I was going to, but then I saw all those pictures and thought maybe you were a lesbian too and that it wouldn't matter. Then that guy Tony started calling, and I figured I was wrong, but I wasn't sure–."

September was quiet for a few moments as Mattie trailed off into silence. She wasn't bothered by the fact that Mattie liked girls. Her and Kate's behavior, as well as why Kate seemed annoyed every time September called her Mattie's friend made sense now. She felt stupid that she hadn't realized before. She was so wrapped up in her fear over telling Mattie about Lizzie, she had missed all the cues. September looked across the room to the framed nude hanging on the wall. "Thanks for telling me. Your art really should have been clued me in."

"Are you okay with this?" Mattie studied her face for a clue to what September was truly feeling. She had been silent since the comment on her artwork.

"Yeah, my uncle's gay. I don't think your girlfriend likes me very much though."

"Kate will be okay. She's not real crazy about me having a girl for a roommate, but she'll get over it once she gets to know you."

"I hope so. Tony's my boyfriend, I guess. We dated at school, and he wants us to keep in touch. He didn't take my moving well." Tony was an area September wanted to avoid. She wasn't sure how she felt about him. Sometimes she thought she loved him, and sometimes she felt like she kept him around so she wouldn't be lonely.

"He seems concerned about you. A lot of people do." Mattie looked like she wanted to say more.

September shifted uncomfortably on the couch. She knew the time had come. "Yeah, well, as long as we're confessing things to each other, I guess I should explain about that."

"You don't have to if you don't want to."

"I know." September paused and twisted the ring on her finger some more. She had made the ring for Lizzie's sixteenth birthday. Her parents had given it back to her before she left for New Mexico. She hadn't taken it off since.

"Is that why you changed schools your senior year, to get away from him?"

"No. Lizzie, the girl in the pictures, was my best friend. We'd known each other since fifth grade. We were roommates at school, and we did everything together." September closed her eyes for a moment and then stared at a point past Mattie's head. *Just say it.* "She died last May."

Mattie placed a comforting hand on September's arm. "I fell apart after Lizzie died. My parents took me to a therapist who thought it would be a good idea if I switched schools. I agreed since I couldn't stand the thought of going back to school and expecting to see her everywhere. You know I'd never even seen the campus before I got here? My parents got some brochures, and I picked here because it was someplace no one I knew had ever heard of."

"I'm so sorry."

"Yeah, me too. I'm on some anti-anxiety medicine and I'm seeing a counselor. There's more to the story, but I don't want to talk about it right now."

Mattie looked at September hesitantly for a moment. "I know this is going to sound bizarre, but can I take your picture?"

"You mean now?" September really didn't want to pose for Mattie, but she was afraid if she said no, Mattie would think she didn't mean it when she said she didn't care that Mattie was a lesbian. She really didn't care who Mattie loved, that was between Mattie and Kate. All she really wanted to do was shut herself in her room and cry. What she had left out was that it had been her fault Lizzie died. Talking about her brought it all back. Looking at Mattie brought it all back.

"Yeah. I'll put in another movie, and you can watch it. You won't even notice me."

"I guess so. I don't want to take off my clothes though." Her therapist was always telling her it wasn't good to keep herself so closed off from everyone. Maybe this would be a step towards becoming Mattie's friend. September smoothed her long, gauzy, black skirt and ran a hand through her hair. "Should I move, or switch positions or something?"

"No, just stay right like you are." Mattie hurried into her studio and came back with her camera. She slipped another movie into the VCR and sat down on the floor beside the couch. She waited for September to become engrossed in the new film before beginning.

Mattie quietly and slowly moved around September, snapping pictures. Occasionally, she moved a piece of her hair, shifted her skirt, or asked her to lift her chin or turn her head, but mostly silently took photographs. Finally, Mattie stopped in front of September. "Will you unbutton your shirt at the bottom for me?"

"Just at the bottom? September hesitated slightly before unbuttoning the last three buttons.

"One more button." Mattie snapped a picture as September did as she asked. "Now, let your shirt fall open at the bottom. Put your right hand on your stomach and your other hand behind your head." Mattie adjusted September's necklace and snapped some more photos. "No, don't look at me. Tilt your head more towards the television. That's good. Bend your right leg a little more." Mattie put her camera down and pushed September's skirt higher up on her legs.

"Mattie, darling, I need your help choosing some photos for that assignment."

Both Mattie and September jumped at the sound of the door opening. September stared as a petite, thin blond in a black miniskirt, high heeled boots and dark red lipstick walked in carrying a six-pack of beer and her black portfolio case.

"Oops. Didn't mean to interrupt, Mattie. Does Kate know you're playing doctor with the new girl?" The blond eyed September's bare stomach with blatant interest. Her stare made September feel naked.

"Angel, I'm working. September, this is Angel. Sometimes the tactful part of her brain shuts down." Mattie looked pointedly at Angel. She shrugged and flashed Mattie another smile as she pulled a joint out of her pocket and lit it.

September sat up and hastily buttoned her shirt back up. She didn't like the way Mattie's friend was eyeing her. "Nice to meet you."

"September, don't get up."

"Don't stop on my account. I'll just sit quietly in the corner till she's done. I enjoy watching Mattie work. It's very–stimulating." Angel smiled and took a hit. Her heavily made-up eyes glittered as they settled on September's still exposed legs.

"No, that's okay. I think I'm ready to stop." September gathered up her photo album and soda and went to her room. She was not going to let this girl keep ogling her. She didn't want to be around this new girl at all. Something about Angel made September very uneasy. She hoped Mattie didn't have this girl over very often. Mattie and Angel heard her bedroom door slam.

Angel handed Mattie a beer. "She's cute. Is she family?"

Mattie sighed. "Leave her alone, Angel, and put that out. Come on, let's go into the studio and look at your pictures."

Chapter 5

"Hey, how was your shooting weekend? Did you get any good pictures?" September called from the kitchen when she heard the front door open. Mattie had gone to Albuquerque for the weekend to shoot pictures in the mountains for a nature photography assignment. September had enjoyed the quiet, but she was glad Mattie was home. She created her best work when other people were creating background noise, and she had been having enough trouble getting her creativity to flow since Lizzie had died.

"Heinous. My back is killing me. The girl I hired to be my assistant didn't show so I had to lug my equipment around all weekend. Between that and the four-hour drive home, I am wiped."

Mattie deposited her equipment on the floor in the living room and walked into the kitchen for a drink. She winced as she pulled open the refrigerator door. Mattie grabbed a Blue Sky out of the fridge and drained almost half of the soda in one swallow. She grimaced in pain again when she lowered the can. She set the can on the counter and rolled her shoulders back and then rolled her head around in a circle, trying to stretch out her muscles.

"Have you eaten dinner yet?" September wiped her hands on the dish towel after she finished putting the last roll in a bowl. She was wearing an apron over her black and white print babydoll dress. There was a smudge of flour on her forehead. "I got in the mood to cook, and I made way too much food. It's almost done. You're welcome to join me if you want."

"It smells great. What is it?" Mattie felt her stomach rumble at the smell of food.

"Broccoli lasagna and homemade rolls. There's a fruit salad in the fridge with no apples."

"Sounds good, but for future reference, I like apples." Mattie glanced at September before she sat down in a chair at the table and began rubbing her right shoulder. September often made assumptions about food she liked. It was odd the way she seemed so sure Mattie liked or didn't like something she'd never mentioned. "I'm starving."

"There's enough time before the food's done that I could give you a massage if you want. I took a class in it when my dad hurt his shoulder a couple years ago. I'm pretty good at it." September could tell Mattie was trying to pretend her shoulder didn't hurt as much as it did. She'd signed up for the class after her father had hurt himself moving some of the pieces at her mother's art gallery. She sometimes wished she could give herself a back massage after working on her sculpture for several hours.

"If you give me a massage, I'll do whatever you want." Mattie slipped off the white oversized shirt she was wearing over her gray tank top.

"Why don't you sit down and lean forwards on the table, and I'll go get some oil to help relax your muscles." September went to her room, retrieved the oil, and came back to the living room, and stood behind Mattie at the table.

September poured a small amount of oil onto her palms and began massaging Mattie's neck and shoulders. The scent of lavender, geranium, and something else Mattie couldn't identify immediately began to relax her. Mattie moaned and squirmed a little at her touch. "Is it too much pressure?"

"No, it feels great." Mattie closed her eyes as September continued to knead the muscles in her shoulders and upper arms. She groaned as September found the biggest knot by her shoulder blade and began working it out. "That spot right there. You are so good at this."

"Shh, don't talk." September continued to massage Mattie's back, working her fingers up and down Mattie's spine. They were both so engrossed in the massage, neither one heard the door open.

"Hey lady, when did you get back?" Kate stopped in the doorway when she saw September leaning over Mattie. "What the fuck is going on?"

Kate's blue eyes narrowed with suspicion. Mattie and September hurried to separate. September nervously pushed imaginary strands of hair behind her ears as she glanced sideways at Kate. *Shit.* It was all totally innocent, but this wasn't going to improve how Kate felt about her. No matter what she did, Kate seemed to hate her.

"Hi, babe. Nothing's going on. My shoulder was hurting. I got back about thirty minutes ago." Mattie tried to kiss Kate hello but got her cheek instead of her mouth. Kate was pissed.

"Do you want to join us for dinner? It should be ready. I'll go check on it." September avoided looking at Kate and went to the oven to check the lasagna. Kate and Mattie followed her.

"No, I don't want to eat with you." Kate rolled her eyes. Would this girl ever get it that she was not welcome? She was always watching Mattie with a longing look on her face. Kate knew it was just a matter of time before she went after her girlfriend.

"Mattie, I thought we could go out to eat. I haven't seen you all weekend." Kate shot hateful looks in September's direction as Mattie got herself another drink from the fridge.

"I told September I'd eat with her. Why don't you eat here too? She made broccoli lasagna and bread and everything." Mattie was tired, she didn't want to go anywhere. She didn't feel like fighting with Kate, especially over something that didn't mean anything.

"Mattie, I haven't seen you all weekend. I'd like to spend some time with you alone." Kate flipped her blond hair over her shoulder.

"It's okay, Mattie. There will be plenty of leftovers."

Mattie sighed. This whole jealousy thing was getting ridiculous. It wasn't that Kate was insecure. She was just possessive when it came to her and September for some reason. "You know, it would be a lot better for all of us if you two could get along. My back was hurting, and September was trying to help, that's all, Kate."

"I just don't feel like lasagna, okay?" Kate slipped a hand into Mattie's hair and whispered in her ear. Kate fingered the bottom of Mattie's shirt. September looked away as Kate nibbled on Mattie's ear. Mattie bit her bottom lip and gave in. She had missed Kate this weekend.

"Fine. Let me put on a different shirt and we'll go." Mattie went into her room, and September turned to face Kate. She was tired of all the hostility she was getting from Mattie's girlfriend. She had never done anything to Kate to make her so angry with her. She really liked Mattie and wanted her girlfriend to like her too.

"What can I do, Kate? How can I make you not hate me?"

"I've seen the way you look at Mattie. I know you think she's cute. She's mine, and I'm not giving her up without a fight." Kate's blue eyes flashed angrily. She kept her voice down so Mattie couldn't hear them.

"What?" September was stunned. This was why Kate didn't like her? She thought she was trying to steal Mattie? "Kate, I'm not gay."

"Keep your hands to yourself and we'll get along fine." Kate turned her back on September and followed Mattie to her room. They still hadn't come out by the time September finished her meal and cleaned up the kitchen.

Chapter 6

September was sitting at the kitchen table, working on a sculpture for class, and Mattie was sitting on the sofa working on a photo collage, when Kate burst into the house. Kate slammed the door behind her. September wiped her hands off on the towel she used for cleaning up the clay and took another bite of her Snoball. Mattie took one look at Kate and jumped up to hug her.

"Hey, Babe, what's wrong?"

"I just saw the school's crime report that they show to potential students at recruitment weekends."

"So?" September covered the statue with a damp cloth, sat down on the couch, and gave Kate her attention. It was obvious she wanted to vent about something. She had pulled away from Mattie and was pacing the floor and waving her arms. "I thought the crime rate was low."

"It is. But they always make it look like there was no crime on campus." Kate threw the booklet down on the coffee table and adjusted the claw clip holding her blond hair up.

"According to them, there were no rapes on campus last year. It doesn't say anything about the three girls that were raped at frat houses because they aren't technically on campus. It doesn't mention hate crimes at all. I know a lesbian whose bike tire got slashed, a guy whose dorm door was spray painted with the word faggot, and two straight guys who got thrashed because they've got gay friends."

"Well, can't you complain to the people that printed it? Ask them to include hate crimes or rapes at frat houses or something?" September put the last piece of her Snoball in her mouth and brushed a few flakes of pink coconut off her hands.

"I can, but I don't think they'll listen. Even if they did, it wouldn't do any good for the kids who are coming tomorrow." Kate sighed and dropped down onto the couch beside September.

"I can't believe they can get away with that." She also couldn't believe she and Kate were having an actual conversation. She must really be upset. September picked up the booklet and flipped through it. "It's too bad there isn't any way you can tell them what's been left out."

"Yeah." Mattie sat down on the couch on the other side of Kate and was silent for a minute. She twisted a curl around her finger. Suddenly, she smiled and got up and went into her room. When she came back a moment later, she was carrying a small cardboard box. "If there was something we could do, would you want to?"

Kate looked at the box for a minute, and then jumped up as understanding lit up her face. "Hell yeah. Let's do it."

"What can we do?" September looked at the box in Mattie's hands. She couldn't tell what was in it and she had no idea what they were talking about.

"I have a friend in women's studies. I'll call her and ask for last year's stats for rapes and hate crimes and things like that. I've got some chalk left over from advertising the student art show last year. We can go chalk the sidewalks. Since it's almost ten now, they won't find it until it's too late to get rid of it."

"Call your friend." Kate was still riled up, but now she was smiling.

"I'd like to help. I just need to change clothes." September went to her bedroom and quickly changed out of the clay-stained shorts and shirt she was wearing into a pair of jeans and a black long-sleeved t-shirt. She threw her hair into a ponytail.

All three of them took a few pieces of chalk and walked the short distance to campus. There were enough security lights on campus that they didn't need flashlights. Together, they all chalked by the Student Union and then split up so they could do the Bookstore and Science building at one time. Kate chalked around the Liberal Arts building, Theater and Black Box Theater. Mattie went to chalk the rape and hate crime warnings around the Administration building and the Library.

September was about to start chalking beside the fountain when one of the bike cops began yelling and riding towards her. September froze momentarily, and then switched her chalk to a color she hadn't used yet. Quickly, she scribbled something on the sidewalk and then stood up. The patrol officer stopped his bike beside her.

"What are you doing? It's kind of late to be out on campus, isn't it?" The cop was eyeing the chalk in her hand.

Please let him believe me, please let him believe me. September took a deep breath. "My dog's lost. I bring her to campus to walk her. I thought maybe she'd come back here."

"What about the chalk?" The man got off his bicycle and nodded toward the chalk in her hand.

"One of my roommates gave it to me. She said we should chalk the sidewalks in case someone finds her. See?" September pointed to the ground. She'd managed to write 'Lost Dog, black, Answers to Missy, 505-356-2234.'

The cop looked at her chalking and looked at her doubtfully. "Are you sure that's all you're doing? Someone's been writing all over the sidewalks tonight. Have you–?"

September saw Mattie and Kate coming around the corner of the library. When they saw September standing by the bicycle cop, they froze. September waved at them. "Mattie! Kate! Did you find Missy?"

Mattie frowned at September as they slowly came over to stand by her. "No."

"Are you looking for the dog too?" The cop eyed Mattie and Kate as they came up to them, also carrying chalk.

Kate glanced at September and then back at the man questioning them. She quickly caught on to the story. She was impressed. September was quick when it counted, and she had volunteered to help even though Kate had never been nice to her. "Yes. You haven't seen any dogs running around, have you?"

"No. It's really late. You girls should wait until tomorrow to do this. I know Portales seems like a safe place, but you still shouldn't be running around at night by yourselves." The cop had apparently decided to believe them. He was getting back on his bike.

"You're right, Officer. We'll go straight home. Just keep an eye out, will you? Missy's very important to me. She's a black cocker spaniel." September smiled at the cop and touched his arm, doing her best to look innocent without over-selling it.

"Of course." The cop waved as he rode away. "You girls go straight home."

Mattie, Kate, and September waited until he was out of sight and then dissolved into giggles. They chalked around the fountain, taking turns keeping a look out for the cop on the bike.

It was almost one o'clock in the morning when they got back to the house. After washing the chalk off their hands, they got drinks out of the kitchen and collapsed on the couch, laughing.

Mattie playfully shoved September, batting her eyes and clutching at her arm. "Oh officer! Please find my dog! She's so special!"

Kate laughed some more and then took a deep breath. "Do you really have a dog?"

September got up and went into her room. When she came out, she was carrying a well-loved stuffed cocker spaniel. She tossed the dog to Kate. "Meet Missy. I've had her since I was three."

Mattie started laughing again. She pulled September back onto the couch beside them. "That's great. You're a pro. I almost died when I came around the corner and saw you with that cop!"

"I've never done anything like that before. It was fun." September released her hair from the ponytail before taking another drink of her Diet Pepsi.

"I've chalked for school events, but not something like this. I can't wait to see people's reactions on campus!" Kate leaned against Mattie.

"The administration is going to be so mad." Mattie took a big swig of her drink and let out a loud burp. Kate swatted at her, laughing.

"I give that a six." September laughed. She paused for a moment and then asked, "Do you really think many people will see what we did?"

Mattie and Kate stopped laughing. "I don't know. I hope so. I mean, the crime rate here is low compared to a lot of other places, but things do happen. Women who want to go here should know what happened."

"So, are we going to do this for the next prospective student weekend too?" Kate yawned.

"Do you want to?" Mattie got up and went into the kitchen. She came back with a bag of Doritos.

"Yeah, I do. We'll probably get caught though. They'll be expecting it."

"We can do it anyway." Mattie offered September the bag. She shook her head no. She hated cheese flavored chips. *Lizzie always forgets I hate Doritos.*

"I'll do it if you all will. I have to get back to my homework." September quickly changed back into her work clothes and uncovered the piece she was working on. Mattie sat down on the sofa, watching her and Kate curled up next to her.

"Thanks for helping, September." Kate yawned again and snuggled into the couch, her head in Mattie's lap.

"Thanks for letting me."

September was glad Mattie and Kate had stayed up with her, even though they weren't talking. She really missed having a friend she could tell everything to. With her sister in Oklahoma and Lizzie gone, September often felt like she was alone. Before she left for New Mexico, her therapist kept telling her she needed to get out and join some groups to meet some people, but she just didn't feel like being sociable a lot of the time. She felt like Mattie was becoming a good friend. Even

Kate might become a friend if they had more nights like tonight. What they'd done earlier tonight reminded her of something she and Lizzie might have done together.

Chapter 7

September was done with classes for the week, and she was looking forward to the three-day weekend coming up because of Labor Day. She wanted to get started on the paper due at the end of the month for her Intro to Women's Studies class.

"You have a visitor." Mattie singsonged as she met September at the front door. She smiled amusedly at September's look of confusion. September dropped her backpack into the chair by the wall and looked around the living room. There was no one there. She turned back towards Mattie.

"Where are they?"

Mattie's smile got larger. A dark-haired guy in jeans and cowboy boots was sneaking up behind September. She jumped as hands suddenly covered her eyes and a familiar voice whispered in her ear, "Guess who?"

"Tony? What are you doing here?" September pulled his hands off her eyes and turned to face him. *What was he doing here?* He should be in Oklahoma. This was not a good weekend for a surprise visit.

"I couldn't wait until Thanksgiving to see you and my Friday class was canceled so I decided to come see you." Tony crushed her against him and kissed her. "I miss you."

Mattie was still watching. September could tell Mattie was trying not to laugh. She shot Mattie a murderous look and disentangled herself from Tony. She was annoyed with Mattie for not warning her he was here. She had a paper to work on and now she was going to have to entertain him too. *I wish he wasn't here.* She clamped down on that thought and pushed it away. He was her boyfriend. Of course she wanted him to be here. September sighed to herself and smiled. She should be glad he cared enough to come see her. She hadn't seen him since August, when she'd had to convince him, he didn't need to drive with her to Eastern.

She still remembered the first time she'd seen him. He had been standing in front of one of the paintings in her mom's gallery. He looked so out of place in his cowboy boots and western shirt, she'd thought he was lost. September had gone over to see if she could give him directions and he'd ended up surprising her with his knowledge about abstract art. When he'd asked her out, she'd said yes. He was the first guy who had surprised her like that in a long time.

She pasted a smile on her face, kissed his cheek and took his hand. "It's good to see you too. Have you seen the house?"

"All I really want to do is get settled in and spend some time with you. My bag is in your room." Tony gave her a squeeze.

"I'm really glad you're here, Tony, but I have a paper I have to work on this weekend. You might want to get a hotel room. I'll be up pretty late." *If you stay here, you're going to want my attention all of the time.* She knew how he was. She had tried to write papers while he was hanging out with her before.

"Then I'll watch you work. I just want to be near you." Tony shut the door to her bedroom. He pulled her close and breathed in her scent. September was familiar with the ritual. Tony wanted to have sex. Soon Tony would start kissing her and trying to take off her clothes. "God, I've missed you so much baby."

Tony tilted her face upwards and kissed her eyelids, cheeks and lips. She felt his hands slide from around her waist and begin to unbutton her shirt. "Did you miss me?"

"Of course, I did." September reluctantly kissed him back. She didn't really feel like having sex in the middle of the day, but she was lonely and being close to Tony might help. She let him take off her shirt before backing away from him and lying down on the bed.

"Whose truck's out back?" Angel walked into the house without knocking as usual.

"September's boyfriend is here." Mattie smiled. "Wait till you see him. They could use his picture as the definition of cowboy. I know he's from Oklahoma, but I thought he'd be a little more alternative. They don't look like they belong together."

"Why wait to see him? I can hear him." Angel smiled and stepped closer to the hallway. Mattie realized Angel could hear September and Tony having sex. Embarrassed, Mattie turned on the stereo to drown out the sound. She really hoped September didn't hear her and Kate. The thought had never occurred to her before. "Hey! This was just getting interesting."

Angel disappeared into the hallway. Mattie thought she was going to the bathroom but when she didn't reappear, Mattie went looking for her. Angel was in her studio with her ear up against the wall.

"Angel! That's gross. Come back into the living room." Mattie hissed, trying to be quiet so September and Tony didn't hear them. She grabbed Angel's arm and pulled at it. Angel shrugged her off.

"No." Angel waved Mattie toward the wall. "You've got to hear this. She's faking! She hasn't seen him in how long and she's faking!"

"Angel, it's none of our business." Mattie tried again to get Angel away from the wall, but curiosity got the better of her. "Besides, how can you tell?"

"Please, I've heard her more excited about those coconut things she eats. Besides, I think I know what a woman sounds like when she's excited." Angel smiled seductively and winked at Mattie. Mattie rolled her eyes. Angel was always talking about sex or saying something suggestive. It could be annoying, but Angel always knew how to have a good time, and nobody was better at picking the best photo out of a series than Angel.

"Come on, we're going into the living room and you're not going to say anything when they come out. I mean it." Mattie grabbed Angel's arm and pulled her out of the studio.

"I should go in there and give him some pointers. At the very least I should slip them some E. Bet I could make her scream." Angel winked at Mattie and went into the kitchen to get a drink. Mattie rolled her eyes and shook her head. Sometimes she didn't know why she hung around with Angel. She didn't want to admit it, but it did sound like Angel was right.

Chapter 8

Mattie picked up her camera and snapped some more pictures of the party guests before putting her camera back on the table and going to get a beer out of the kitchen. Most of the pictures probably wouldn't be usable, but she might find one or two good ones out of the roll. She would probably get better ones in a couple of weeks at the Halloween party.

Kate followed her into the small kitchen and gave her a long kiss. "Thanks for hosting the cast party."

"No problem. I still can't believe you managed to talk the director into doing The Crucible set at a Catholic school." Mattie kissed her back. "You're going to stay tonight, aren't you? You look pretty sexy in that plaid skirt." Mattie grabbed a piece of caramel corn out of the plastic bowl on the counter.

"Of course, I'm going to stay." Kate stole one more kiss before getting herself a beer. The tiny plaid skirt and thigh high socks showed off every one of Kate's curves. Mattie couldn't wait to peel them off of her.

Mattie walked back into the living room. "Where did everybody go?"

"It's almost midnight, last call for alcohol at the store."

The party had dwindled down to about ten guests. September was in the corner, talking to a girl she knew from her painting class. Angel appeared from the hallway with a girl dressed in leather and chains following behind her on a leash. The dark red lipstick they were both wearing was smeared and Angel had a bit of white powder on her nose.

"Razor party, Mattie. Let's gather up the guests and play truth or dare." Angel went into the living room and joined the circle of people sitting on the floor. Mattie and Kate joined her. September wandered over to the circle and sat down as Angel pulled out a joint and lit it. She took a deep hit and passed it to the person next to her. September looked around the circle as she passed on the joint without taking a hit. Kate, Mattie, and Angel were sitting next to each other, with Angel's girlfriend and two more girls September knew she had met but couldn't remember their names.

"Mandy, truth or dare?"

"Truth."

"Have you ever been in a threesome?" Gena smiled. She already knew the answer.

"Bitch! I told you that in secret! How could you?"

"I do not get the attraction with threesomes." Mattie rolled her eyes and Kate squeezed her arm.

"Try it and you'll understand. They're fun. I'd be happy to stay tonight and initiate you and Kate." Angel smiled and blew Mattie a kiss.

"No thanks." Mattie shook her head.

September slowly sipped her beer, not paying much attention to the game. Truth or dare was the same no matter who was playing. After a few boring questions, all of the questions started to revolve around sex. September didn't care about the sex lives of people she didn't know. She let her mind wander until she heard Angel say her name.

"Truth or dare, September?" From the wicked smile on Angel's face, September knew either choice was trouble. She didn't understand why Mattie liked Angel. She was a total bitch. With someone like Angel, the truth was probably safer.

"Truth."

"What made you leave OU in your senior year to come to this place?" Angel stared at her with a smug look in her eyes. September stared down at the beer she was holding. She should have known Angel would ask her that. Angel had tried many times to get her to say why she had moved to Portales, but she had never wanted to tell her about Lizzie. September refused to let Angel force her to reveal something so personal in front of a group that was mostly strangers. Angel didn't deserve to know about Lizzie. If she told her what had happened, September knew Angel would find ways to bring it up and sneak it into conversation every chance she got. No matter what the dare was, it had to be better than answering the truth question.

"I'll take the dare." September met Angel's stare. Angel's blue eyes glittered cruelly; she licked her lips before answering.

"I dare you to kiss the person in this circle you're most attracted to." Angel's smile was predatory. She knew September wouldn't answer the truth question and everyone in the circle was female.

September let her eyes travel over the faces in the circle. She refused to kiss someone she didn't know, and Angel and her girlfriend were out of the question. She wouldn't give Angel the satisfaction and anyone who would voluntarily let Angel lead them around by a dog leash had serious issues. That only left Kate or Mattie, and either one would make Kate livid. If she refused to play the game at this point, Angel would never let her live it down. She briefly considered telling Angel about Lizzie one more time, but quickly dismissed it. She couldn't let Angel weaponize Lizzie against her.

"Angel, that's not fair! You know September isn't-." Mattie protested.

"It was a simple truth question. She chose to go for the dare instead. So, who's it going to be?"

Everyone was staring at her. One of the girls she didn't know giggled. September moved across the circle until she was right in front of Angel. Angel smiled and licked her lips. September took Mattie's drink from her and handed both her and Mattie's drinks to Angel. She smiled at the look of surprise on Angel's face. "Hold these for a minute."

September searched Mattie's face for a moment for a clue to what she was thinking. She really hoped Mattie didn't mind. She suddenly realized she was nervous about kissing Lizzie. *Why am I nervous?* It was just a silly dare in a game. She closed her eyes and slowly leaned in, giving Mattie a small, tentative kiss.

She was surprised at how soft Mattie's lips were. It was different than kissing Tony. She kissed her again and felt Mattie's hand slide under her hair and pull her into a longer kiss. She returned Mattie's kiss, biting gently at Mattie's full lower lip before opening her mouth to let Mattie's darting tongue slide across her own. *This is nice.*

Mattie suddenly let go of her as Kate stood up, pushed past them, running towards Mattie's bedroom and Angel began applauding. Mattie stood up and hurried after Kate. September sat still, stunned at her reaction to Mattie's kiss.

"Can I be next?" Angel winked at September.

"Fail to be a bitch, Angel." September grabbed her beer from Angel and took a big drink. She couldn't quite bring herself to look at Angel. She'd stood up to Angel by not backing out of the dare, but somehow it still felt like Angel had won.

"What the hell was that?" Kate's voice sliced through the tense silence in the living room.

"Well, that's my cue to bounce. Party's over." Angel said as the sounds of Kate and Mattie's argument drifted into the living room. The guests quickly began to filter out of the house. One blond girl hesitated like she wanted to say something to September but left instead as the argument got even louder. September stayed on the floor in the living room for a few minutes after it emptied out, staring at the mess left over from the party.

She got up and half-heartedly began collecting beer cans and trash but gave up after a few moments. She dropped the garbage bag and sat down on the couch. September kept thinking about how much she had enjoyed Mattie's kiss. It was so much gentler than Tony's kisses. She wandered over to Mattie's bookcase and began looking over the books. For the first time, she really noticed the titles. They're mostly lesbian novels, she realized. *Rubyfruit Jungle, I've heard of this one.* September took it off the shelf. She looked at it for a moment and then took it into her room and turned on the stereo to try and drown out Mattie and Kate's voices.

September looked up, startled, when her bedroom door opened and Kate burst into her room, Mattie following behind her. She grabbed her English book beside her on the bed and used it to cover up the book she'd borrowed from Mattie. "Kate? What are you doing in here?" Kate had never set foot inside her room before and September couldn't imagine that this was a good sign.

"We need to talk." Kate pulled herself up to her full five-foot four-inch height and stood staring at September with her arms crossed over her chest. Her blue eyes were blazing, and September knew they were about to have it out. She decided to try and head Kate off by apologizing immediately. Regardless of how much she liked Mattie's kiss, she never should have kissed her since neither one of them were single. Especially not in front of Kate.

September sighed and sat up. "Listen, Kate, I'm really sorry."

"You should be. Mattie's my girlfriend." Kate wasn't about to let her off the hook easily.

"Kate, stop it." Mattie shifted her weight from one bare foot to the other. She looked embarrassed. She ran a hand through her hair and glanced apologetically at September.

"No, Mattie, it's okay. I really am sorry. I had too much to drink and I wasn't thinking. I should have just answered the question."

"Not if you didn't want to. Angel is my friend, but she can be a real bitch sometimes." Mattie just wanted this all to be resolved. She was tired and wanted to sleep. Kate was staying the night, but instead of having sex, they'd be fighting all night.

"I'm sorry, Kate. It's just that Mattie was the only person there I felt comfortable kissing. I know she's your girlfriend and I overstepped my boundaries. I shouldn't have done that to you or to Tony."

"Don't lie to me, September. I know there's more to it than that."

"No, there's not." September frowned.

"September, I caught you massaging Mattie, you're constantly staring at her with this look on your face like you want her, and that kiss was pretty familiar. I don't think that's the first time you've kissed her."

"Kate, we've been over this. I'm not cheating on you! September's straight, there's nothing going on." Mattie tried to pull Kate out of the room, but Kate shrugged her off.

"She may have you fooled, but not me. We both know you're not straight, don't we, September? Does your girlfriend know you're cheating on her?"

September frowned at Kate, puzzled by her question. *This girl was nuts!* She looked at Mattie, who shrugged her shoulders and shook her head. "What the hell are you talking about, Kate? I don't have a girlfriend. Mattie's right, I'm not gay. I told you that."

"Please! You've got pictures of that girl all over the place!" Kate waved her arm towards the picture of Lizzie on September's dresser. "Am I really supposed to believe she's not your girlfriend? Don't think I haven't noticed the resemblance."

"Kate, she's not." Mattie touched Kate's arm and Kate pulled away. September looked at the pictures on her dresser, and then back at Kate. She had had enough. She wasn't going to let Kate stand in the middle of her room and accuse her of things she hadn't done any longer.

"Kate, I do not have to explain myself to you. I've apologized and I've told you that I do not have a girlfriend and I'm not interested in Mattie. I think you should leave my room now." September was not going to explain about Lizzie to Kate while she was being like this.

"I'm not leaving until you tell me the truth!" Kate stomped her foot.

"Kate, that's enough. Let's go. We are telling you the truth." Mattie tried to pull Kate out of September's room. Kate jerked away.

"Don't think I didn't notice that you kissed her back, Mattie! We will be discussing that." Kate glared at Mattie and then looked back at September. "Give me her phone number. If you're telling me the truth, you won't mind giving me her phone number so I can call her for myself."

"Kate, stop it now." Mattie's voice suddenly sounded angry enough to make Kate look away for the first time. "I mean it, Kate. Stop it."

Mattie knew how uncomfortable September was talking about Lizzie, and she wasn't going to let Kate force her to discuss it if she didn't want to. Especially if it was because she had made the mistake of getting carried away while playing a game. Mattie was convinced it was her fault the kiss had gone on as long as it had. It never occurred to her that September could have ended it if she'd wanted to.

"I'm not giving you her phone number. Now, please leave my room." September was dangerously close to losing her temper. Kate was one of the most stubborn people she'd ever met. This conversation was giving her a headache. She just wanted to take some Advil and go to bed.

"If you don't have anything to hide, you shouldn't mind giving me her phone number."

September stood up. Like Mattie and Kate, September had changed into her pajamas. Her long legs were bare under her nightgown and Mattie could see she was shaking. "Mattie, get her out of here."

"September, I want her phone-."

"I can't give you her phone number! She's dead! Now get out!" September yelled, shaking with rage.

"I-I-." Kate looked stunned.

"Get out!" September grabbed a stuffed animal off her bed and threw it at Kate. She ducked and let Mattie pull her out of the room. September slammed the bedroom door behind them so hard the mirror over her dresser shook. She sat down and rubbed her temples.

What the hell was Kate thinking? The idea of her and Mattie or her and Lizzie together was ridiculous. She had liked the kiss, but that didn't mean anything. She and Lizzie had kissed hello and hugged each other all the time. They'd even slept in the same bed sometimes. It didn't mean anything. It was just the way their friendship worked.

September was upset. Who did Kate think she was to accuse her of sneaking around? Even if she had dated Lizzie, she never would have cheated on her. That just wasn't in her nature. September hugged the tattered stuffed dog she'd had since she was a baby as tears started rolling down her cheeks. She would give anything to be able to call Lizzie one more time.

She threw the dog down and wiped at her cheeks when she heard the door open. Mattie sat down on the bed beside her and put an arm around her. "Are you okay?"

September started to nod but burst into sobs when Mattie hugged her. "I don't know. I'm so sorry, I didn't mean to-I just couldn't tell Angel. She really hates me now."

Mattie rubbed her hand up and down September's back. It reminded her of Spring. Her sister used to rub her back when she had trouble sleeping or was upset. "Kate doesn't hate you. She's upset with me. She wanted us to move in together and I said no. You moved in two weeks later. She's jealous you're living with me."

"I really want to get along with her. I hate it that she doesn't like me." September wiped at the tear tracks on her cheeks. "What can I do?"

"It doesn't matter. You don't have to do anything." Mattie let go of September and ran a hand through her dark curls. She fiddled with a button on her nightshirt. "We just broke up."

"What? Not because of me." September was stunned. Mattie and Kate seemed so happy most of the time.

"Not because of you. She's possessive and this thing with accusing you and me of cheating is so stupid. I'm tired of it." Mattie squirmed and reached under her to see what she was sitting on. "She's always at rehearsal lately anyway."

September's eyes widened as Mattie pulled the book she had borrowed from underneath the pillow. She tried to grab it before Mattie could see the title, but Mattie held it out of her reach. "What's this?"

"It's nothing. I was looking for something to read and I saw it on your shelf. It's okay if I borrow it, isn't it?"

"Of course. You can borrow any book you want." Mattie paused. "You know that book is-."

"I know. You're sure you don't mind?" September was feeling better about the scene with Kate, but she was beginning to feel extremely uncomfortable about where this conversation was headed. She faked a yawn. "I'm really tired. I'll talk to you in the morning, okay?"

"Sure. See you in the morning." Mattie gave September one more look she couldn't quite interpret before closing the door behind her.

Chapter 9

It had been two weeks since the party where Mattie and Kate had broken up. Kate had called and apologized to Mattie, but they had both agreed it was over. Mattie had been spending a lot of time at Angel's working on a photography project. September had finished Mattie's book and read a couple more she'd found on the shelves. For the first time, Mattie was actually home, and September went to find her.

"Hey, what are you up to?" September stood in the doorway of Mattie's studio. It had taken her ten minutes just to work up the courage to step inside.

"I'm hanging some new pictures. Do you want to see them?"

"Sure." September came into the room and stood beside Mattie. She looked at the series of photographs Mattie pointed out. The three-photo series of a woman sleeping and then staring sleepy-eyed into the camera was beautiful. September gasped as she finally realized why the fresh-faced woman looked familiar. "Is that Angel? She looks so different."

"Yeah." Mattie put a hand on her arm. "Come over here. I never showed you the ones I took of you." Mattie stood behind September with her hands on her shoulders. September tried to concentrate on the photos but had trouble paying attention to anything but the warmth of Mattie's hands through her shirt. She took a deep breath to try and calm herself. Thoughts of Tony popped into her head. September shook her head to clear it. She might lose her nerve if she thought of him right now.

If you're going to do this, do it, she told herself. You put on the shorts and shirt she said she'd like to photograph you in, so do it. September turned around. Mattie was so close they were still touching. "I thought about it, and I want to pose for you." She paused and took a deep breath. "However you want me to."

"Really?" Mattie took a step back. She was thrilled, but September looked like she was about to bolt so she tried to stay calm. "Right now?"

"If you want to now, that's fine." September watched as Mattie pulled a chair into the middle of the room and turned on some lights. When Mattie gestured to the chair, September walked over to it and sat down. She was shaking inside. She straddled the chair like Mattie instructed. The back of the chair was low; it only came up to the bottom of her ribcage.

After a few pictures, September unbuttoned her shirt partway and exposed her right shoulder, bracing herself for Mattie's reaction. There was a raised, slightly jagged, diagonal scar about two and a half inches long running from the outer edge of September's collarbone down towards her breast. It was still slightly red and puffy. Mattie froze momentarily at the sight of her scar but didn't say anything. Without waiting for Mattie to ask her, September slowly unbuttoned her shirt all the way. Mattie murmured encouragement and kept taking pictures.

"I've got to reload the film. After I do that, let's get some with your shirt off." Mattie's eyes darted to her scar and back to September's eyes, trying to make sure she was comfortable with the situation. The scar made the pictures better in Mattie's mind. September's scar was proof that beauty didn't have to be perfect to be real. "Is that okay?"

September stared back at her and nodded. She waited until Mattie was looking at her, and slowly slid the button-down shirt off her shoulders, watching as Mattie fiddled with her camera and bit her lower lip. The bra she was wearing underneath the shirt was lacey and not quite see-through.

"I'm going to do some close-ups now, okay?" Mattie put down her camera and approached September. "I'm just going to arrange your hair the way I want it for these next few shots."

"Okay." September closed her eyes and took a deep breath as she felt Mattie begin to play with her hair. Just as she was about to turn around and take Mattie's hand, Mattie went back to her camera. Mattie walked around the back of September, taking pictures. September resisted the urge to turn her head and see what Mattie was doing.

"I'm going to have to move your bra strap to get the picture I want." September reached up to push her strap down and brushed Mattie's hand. They both jerked their hands away. September reached back up and slid the strap down her shoulder. Mattie cleared her throat and tried taking the picture again. "Can you get it any lower? It's still in the shot."

"I can take it off if you want." September's voice sounded too loud in her ears. She started to reach behind her to unhook it, but Mattie stopped her.

"I'll get it." Mattie unhooked September's bra. September hoped Mattie hadn't noticed her breathing had quickened. September slid her bra off and threw it over by her shirt. "I need to fix your hair again."

Mattie's hands in her hair felt good. September turned her head to look at Mattie. Mattie stared into her eyes for a moment. September lifted her hand to touch Mattie's cheek but quickly dropped it back to her side. *What am I doing?* I can't kiss her, I'm half-naked. She's going to think I want to do more than kiss her.

September took a deep breath as she finally admitted to herself the reason she wanted to pose for Mattie. She turned her head away from Mattie to hide the flush she felt creeping into her cheeks.

"I'm getting cold."

"Oh, of course. I'm sorry. I only have a couple more shots, okay?" Mattie backed away and picked up her camera. She took a few more pictures before telling September she was finished. Mattie kept her back turned towards September as she took the film from the camera and left the room.

September put her clothes back on and sat in the room for a few minutes, trying to digest what she had just realized. She wanted Mattie to kiss her again. September studied some of the photos on the wall of women kissing each other and was surprised again at how much the pictures appealed to her. *I've got to get out of here*, September thought. It's just being in here that's making me feel like this. I just need to get out of the house for a while.

September went to her room, grabbed her backpack and keys, and headed towards the door. She was stopped in the doorway to the living room by the sight of Mattie and Angel on the couch. Angel had an arm around Mattie and was kissing her. September stood watching for a moment. She and Kate had only been broken up for a week. When did this happen? She walked through the room, secretly pleased when Mattie pulled away from Angel. "Sorry, didn't mean to interrupt."

September shut the front door behind her, trying to ignore what she was afraid was a stab of jealousy. Why on earth would she be jealous? September quickly shoved the thought out of her head before she could think about what it might really mean. Maybe the pottery studio would have a wheel open.

The whir of the pottery wheel and the feel of the clay under her nails were lulling September into a trance-like state. Her mother had been right. She had suggested to September, the last time they had talked, that to try and break through her creative block, she should go back to the basics. September had decided to try it and had lucked into one of the pottery wheels in the art department being free. She'd been able to get out of her head and she'd already thrown two vases and a bowl. If this vase turned out like she thought it was going to, she was going to give it to her mother when she was through.

She was so engrossed in her work; she didn't hear the door open. September didn't notice Tom, the photography professor, standing in front of her until she stopped and reached for the wire she used to remove pieces from the wheel. He waited until she had placed the vase on the drying table next to her before he spoke.

"How's Mattie doing?" Tom was leaning against the metal lockers that lined one wall of the studio.

"She's okay, I guess. Why?" September knew who Tom was, she'd met him a couple of times with Mattie, but they'd never really had a conversation. She wasn't sure why he had decided to seek her out.

"She hasn't been in class lately. I thought maybe she was sick." Tom shifted his position and moved closer to look at September's work. "These are nice."

"Thanks." September shrugged. They weren't anywhere close to the kind of work she could do. They were good enough to turn in for class. Her grades weren't as important to her as making it through school. "Mattie isn't sick. I'm sure she'll be in class tomorrow."

"I hope so. She's missed an entire week. If she misses much more, she'll never catch up." Tom handed September a paper towel to dry her hands with. "Tomorrow's the last day to register for the Adams competition. Mattie's the best student I've got. She has a real shot if she gets her portfolio in. Winning a contest like that can do a lot for a photographer's career. She knows she needs to enter this."

"I'll remind her when I see her. I know she's been collecting photos for something. Maybe it was that." September began cleaning up her workspace. She still had almost forty-five minutes, but she didn't feel like throwing anymore. She was lying to Tom, and she wasn't really sure why. She hadn't seen Mattie collecting any photos lately. It wasn't really her business if Mattie had decided not to enter the contest Tom was talking about. God, she hated lying. She put her pieces with the others on the drying table and collected her things.

She would mention what Tom had said when Mattie got home tonight. September sighed. She was doing it again. She used to cover for Lizzie with her professors too, only then she didn't know what was going on. No more lying for Mattie, she promised herself. It's not my responsibility to make sure she meets her deadlines. If she wants to skip classes and blow off this competition, it's none of my business.

Chapter 10

September couldn't wait to get home. She loved the couple of hours she had to herself every Thursday afternoon before Mattie got home from class. She was going to put some music on, find a good book, and take a long, hot bath with absolutely no interruptions. Hopefully, Mattie had gone to class today. In the month that Mattie had been dating Angel, it was hard to tell whether she was going to be home or at class.

"Not again." September sighed as she opened the door. The living room reeked of marijuana. Why anyone wanted to smoke something that smelled like someone with terrible body odor had put on a dirty shirt and gone out into the hot sun to exercise for five hours escaped September. She dropped her backpack onto the floor beside the front door, picked her way across the cluttered floor, and quickly opened all four of the living room windows. The mess was all Mattie's things. She never cleaned up after herself anymore.

Mattie was passed out on the couch in the same clothes she'd been wearing yesterday. September took a deep breath to calm the flash of panic that still came every time she saw Mattie like this. She checked to make sure Mattie was breathing and went into the kitchen for the Febreze. She sprayed the living room with almost half the bottle. Thankfully, the door to her room was still closed. She went in and checked. It did smell a little, so she sprayed her room too and went back into the kitchen. She put the bottle back under the kitchen sink and sighed when she saw the condition of the kitchen. Mattie had gotten the munchies.

September pulled the trash can over to the table. She began sweeping empty soda and beer cans and wrappers into it. She picked up one of the wrappers and sighed. Mattie had finished her Snoballs. She was not going to wash Mattie's dirty dishes. She picked up the plates and silverware and put them in the sink. She put the bottle of juice back in the refrigerator. The leftovers she was going to eat for dinner were gone too. *Take out for dinner it is.* She grabbed a soda from the fridge and went into her bedroom.

Sitting down on her bed, she opened her Diet Pepsi and sighed. She couldn't keep this up much longer. Mattie was driving her crazy. She never knew whether Mattie was going to be in class, or eat all her food, or if the house was going to stink like weed when she got home. This was all Angel's influence. September had thought she'd seen Angel passing out drugs a few times at parties, but she'd never been sure. Now she was. Mattie was never like this when she was dating Kate. Had it been this bad when she lived with Lizzie? September couldn't remember. Lizzie had always been messy, and she'd been better at hiding her drug habit.

September took another drink of her soda. Maybe Kate could help her convince Mattie to tone down the partying. September laughed out loud and shook her head. Kate hated her. She would never agree to help her, but she probably still cared about Mattie. She might do it if it meant helping Mattie. Maybe. September changed into her robe and found her book. She might not be alone, but she definitely needed her bath more than ever. Who cared if the stereo bothered Mattie? September was tired of taking care of Lizzie. She turned on the stereo and went into the bathroom, locking the door behind her.

September had finished her bath and decided to make herself some dessert. She put it in the fridge to chill and sat down on the couch to read. Mattie must have woken up while she was in the bathtub. She hadn't been on the couch when she'd come out.

"This is great! What is it?" Mattie stuck her finger in the lemon custard September had made and pulled it out of the refrigerator to spoon some into a bowl.

"Spoon some of the strawberry sauce on top." She knew what Mattie was into without looking. It was the only thing in the refrigerator that didn't need to be heated up. September was sitting on the couch, reading another one of the books she had borrowed from Mattie's shelf. She heard Mattie dig in the refrigerator some more before heading into the living room.

"Wanna watch a movie?"

"Sure."

September needed to study, but it had been so long since she and Mattie had spent any time together, she was willing to put it off. She wasn't even sure what movie Mattie had in mind for them. Mattie sat down beside her.

"I've got *Dazed and Confused*, or *Girl, Interrupted*. Which one do you want to watch first?"

September didn't want to watch either one of them. One was a drug movie and the other one hit way too close to home. She couldn't believe Mattie had thought she'd want to watch either of these movies. She wanted to spend time with her, but not by watching these movies. Right after Lizzie's death, she had watched *Girl, Interrupted* over and over until she had destroyed the tape in a fit of panic that she might belong in a place like that hospital. That was when she started seeing a therapist and she hadn't watched that movie since.

"I don't care. Why don't you pick? I'm at a really good part in this book, I might just sit here with you and try to finish it."

"I wanted to watch a movie with you. We haven't spent time together in a long time." Mattie ate the last bite of her custard in her bowl and put the spoon on the table. "What book are you reading?"

September partially closed the book and showed Mattie the front cover. Mattie stared at it for a moment, grabbed the book out of her hand, and hit her with it. September threw her hands up to protect herself. "Hey!"

"What the hell are you doing with my book? I've been looking for this! Haven't you ever heard of asking before you take other people's stuff?"

September stared at Mattie in confusion. She had changed from her friend to someone she didn't know in the blink of an eye. Why was it such a big deal to Mattie that she was reading one of her books? She had told September she could borrow any of them she wanted to. She scooted away from Mattie on the couch as she grabbed her bowl and threw it across the room.

"I'm sorry. You said I could borrow your books if I wanted to. I didn't mean to take the one you were using."

"I meant you could borrow them if you asked first. Don't ever touch my things without asking!" Mattie threw the book on the sofa, grabbed her jacket and stormed out of the house. September stared after her, confused as to what had just happened.

Mattie's mood swings were becoming more frequent lately. September was never sure when the littlest thing would set her off. This was the first time she had become violent. September rubbed her face with her hand. She knew what she had to do. She had to talk to Kate. This had to be drugs. She was sure Mattie was using more than weed. Pot wouldn't make her behavior this erratic. It would account for her sleeping in and not going to class, but not the mood swings or violence. Maybe Kate could help her find out what exactly was going on. She knew more of Mattie and Angel's mutual friends than September did. She went to her room to start on her homework. She knew if she checked the theater rehearsal space tomorrow, she would either find Kate, or find out when she would be there.

Chapter 11

"What are you doing here?" Kate lifted her leg off the barre and stared at September in the doorway of the dance studio. September was the one person Kate had never expected to see again. She had thought about finding her to apologize, she hadn't known her friend had died, but had decided against it. Kate still partially blamed September for Mattie dumping her.

"I need to talk to you." September tucked a piece of hair behind her ear and nervously licked her lips. Not sure if she should step on the wooden floor with her shoes, she stayed in the doorway.

"I'm getting ready to go into rehearsal." Kate lifted her other leg onto the wooden barre attached to the wall and gracefully leaned over it in a stretch, touching the fingers of her left hand to her toes.

"Kate, please. It's important." September knew it would be hard to get Kate to talk to her, but she hadn't considered the possibility that Kate would refuse. She didn't know whom else to get advice from.

"I'm busy, September, and I don't have anything to say to you. Now please let me finish stretching."

A tall, thin girl in a black leotard and tights, with her brown hair up in a bun identical to Kate's, appeared in the doorway behind September. "Kate, it's our turn."

Kate gathered her things and brushed past September. She followed Kate and the other girl down the hall. Kate dropped her black nylon bag on the floor beside the door to the stage and went inside without another glance at September. September sat down on the worn-out gray couch beside the door to wait for Kate to come back out. She had to get Kate to listen to her. The other students in the green room looked at her briefly before going back to their studies or rehearsals.

"See you tomorrow, Kate." Kate and the six other dancers in the show came out of the stage door. Kate pulled jeans and a blue sweater out of her bag and put them on over her tights and leotard.

"Hey, your friend is still here." Kate turned around to see September asleep on the green room couch. Kate sighed.

"Shit." Kate walked over to the couch and nudged September's leg with her foot. "Hey, September, wake up."

September sat up, rubbing her eyes. "Kate? Can you talk now?" She hadn't meant to fall asleep, but she'd been so worried lately she hadn't been sleeping well.

"Yes. Come on, they're waiting on us to lock up."

September stood and followed Kate out the door and to her car. "Can I buy you some coffee?"

Kate threw her bag into the backseat of her red Volkswagen bug and turned to stare at September for a moment. She did look worried about something. Kate sighed.

"You really waited three hours just to talk to me?"

"It's important. I'm worried about Mattie." September pulled her coat tighter around her as the wind blew her long skirt up around her knees and looked past Kate. She decided to get it all out in the open. "I didn't know where else to go."

"What makes you think I care what happens to Mattie?" Kate couldn't quite manage to look September in the eye.

"Because I think you still care about her." September stared into Kate's blue eyes, daring her to deny it. Kate was silent for a moment, then sighed.

"Get in." The two-minute drive to the diner was silent.

Kate dipped her cheese fry into the cream gravy before popping it into her mouth. She'd regret it later when she was working it off, but this conversation was going to require greasy carbs, she just knew it. "I don't understand why you're so freaked out. Mattie's always known how to party hard. I know you've seen her do it."

"But not like this. Now that she's dating Angel, it's different." September squirmed on the cracked red vinyl booth. They were sitting in the corner of the diner, as far away from the other students studying for tests and couples unwilling to end their dates as they could get.

Kate paused, her cup halfway to her mouth. "Her and Angel?" Kate took a gulp of her coffee and winced as it scalded her throat on the way down. "When did that start?" She didn't quite control the shaking of her hand as she set the mug down.

"The end of October, I think." September pulled one of the cheese fries off the plate and ate it, ignoring the bowl of cream gravy on the table.

"Are you sure?" Kate's voice was soft. She drew circles with her fingers in some spilled sugar on the table. Even though Kate knew Mattie was right about them breaking up, she didn't want to hear that Mattie was dating someone else already.

"Yeah. I walked in on them making out once, and Angel isn't exactly as quiet as you were, if you know what I mean." September made a face.

"Um, yeah, I do." Kate stared down at the table.

"She's different now. Mattie's not going to class, and she isn't taking photographs anymore. All she does is hang around the house."

"Maybe she just needs a break." Kate shrugged.

"I don't think so." September shook her head. She signaled to the waitress for more coffee.

Kate leaned back in the booth. "I think you're overreacting. I don't know what else to tell you. It's none of our business. Mattie's a big girl. It's her life."

September sighed and looked down. She looked out the window of the diner and toyed with her cup. She had to make Kate understand.

"I really think it's nothing, September."

"I don't know, Kate. It's just-Mattie's my best friend here and I don't want to lose her, you know?"

Kate sighed. "Yeah, I understand. I just don't think you have anything to worry about. If you're really that concerned, I guess I can ask around and see what I can find out."

September was quiet for a moment and then made up her mind to tell Kate everything. "I'd appreciate it. It's not just the way she's acting."

"What do you mean?" Kate looked puzzled.

"I-I take anti-anxiety medication, and-."

"Because of your friend?" Kate's voice softened as she remembered what September had admitted after the party. "I really was an idiot that night. I'm sorry about that."

"It's okay. I'm sorry too." September took a deep breath. "Anyway, a week ago I got my prescription filled. Yesterday I went to take one and I couldn't find the bottle."

"Maybe you lost it?"

"Kate, I always put it in the same place. I searched the house. It's gone. I looked everywhere." September waved the waitress away when she tried to refill her cup again. Kate glanced quickly at the woman, shook her head no, and returned her attention back to September.

"Did you ask Mattie about it?"

"She said she hadn't seen it. I don't think she was lying, but with the way she's been acting lately, I just don't know."

"That is kind of strange. You're sure you didn't lose it?"

September looked exasperated. "Kate, it's a seventy-five-dollar prescription! I didn't lose it. I put it on my dresser and now it's gone." Kate opened her mouth to say more, but September stopped her with a glare. "I didn't drop it on the floor, I didn't put it in my purse, I didn't leave it in the kitchen or in my car. I didn't lose it."

"I believe you." Kate sighed. She couldn't believe Mattie would get involved with drugs like September was suggesting. She grabbed a napkin and wrote her phone number on it. "Call me if anything else happens and I'll ask around, okay?"

"Thanks." September signaled the waitress for the check.

Chapter 12

"September, it's two o'clock in the morning! What is so important?" Kate demanded as she entered the house. She and September had started getting along and spending more time together since their talk at the diner, but she hadn't expected September to take her up on her offer to call her in the middle of the night. She was wearing a sweater and jeans and looked like she'd just crawled out of bed, which she had. Her blond hair was thrown into a ponytail at the top of her head.

September was sitting on the couch in her nightgown. She was nervously clasping and unclasping her hands. She had never been so glad to see Kate. Any doubts she had about Mattie's drug use were gone. She couldn't deal with this on her own. "Go look in the kitchen."

Unable to sit still, she got up from the sofa and followed Kate to the doorway of the kitchen. Kate stopped and gripped the side of the door frame for support. She shook her head as if to clear her vision. The kitchen looked like a tornado had hit it.

All of the cabinet doors and most of the drawers were open. Dishes were piled on the counters, the stove and on every surface there was room for them. Mattie was standing in front of the sink, frantically scrubbing some plates with a piece of steel wool. The water in the sink was so hot, steam was rising from the bubbles. Mattie wasn't wearing rubber gloves. Her hands were red and raw looking. Water was splashed all over her jeans and shirt.

"Mattie, what are you doing?"

"The dishes aren't clean enough. I can't see myself in them. They have to be clean. We eat off them and they aren't clean!" Mattie's voice was higher and sharper than usual. She was speaking so rapidly Kate was having a hard time understanding her.

"Aren't the dishes in the cabinet supposed to be clean?"

"They're supposed to be, but they aren't. Look at them! They don't look clean enough to me." Mattie went back to scrubbing the plates in the sink with her steel wool. Kate turned to face September.

"How long has she been like this?"

September sighed. "I don't know. She woke me up when she was pulling all of the dishes out of the cabinets. That was about forty-five minutes ago." September walked back to the couch and sat down, pulling a blanket around her. Kate sat down beside her. "I can't get her to stop. I can't convince her the dishes are clean. It's like she's got a one-track mind."

"Speed."

"What?"

Kate looked down at her hands for a moment and then back at September. "I should have listened to you at the diner. You were right. She's on speed. There was a dancer last year that was using it. She's going to keep going till she crashes."

"So, what can we do? I have a test tomorrow morning. I have to get some sleep but I'm afraid she's going to hurt herself. Did you see her hands?"

Kate thought for a moment. She looked around the living room and finally her eyes landed on the bookcase. She walked over to it and began pulling some of the books off the shelves and scattering them in various places around the living room. Kate motioned her to come and help. September stood but remained by the couch.

"She's going to keep going but maybe we can get her to do something quiet. Maybe we can convince her that the bookcase needs to be dusted and the books need to be rearranged."

"Okay." September looked doubtful. She grabbed a few of the paperbacks off the top shelf and coughed as dust fell into her face. They did need to be dusted. Abandoning the books, September pulled the videos out of the cabinet under the television and scattered them on the floor. "Kate, did you ever ask around about Angel and the drugs?"

Kate froze and didn't look at September for a few moments. Finally, she nodded. "Are you going to tell me what you heard?"

"Not tonight, but yes." Kate put her handful of books down on the coffee table. Kate started towards the kitchen. September followed her, hoping they could convince Mattie to attack the living room instead.

"Lizzie, have you seen-?" At the sound of September's voice Mattie's hands flew up to her ears and she turned around.

"Shhhh! Don't talk! I can't stand the sound of your voice!" Mattie's pupils were dilated, and her skin was flushed.

"Mattie, I don't understand." September looked confused. She stepped back in fear as Mattie started towards her, hands outstretched.

"Don't talk! Don't say anything!" Mattie stopped her advance on September when she nodded and put a hand over her mouth. Kate's eyes darted from Mattie to September, and she stepped in between them.

"Mattie, have you seen the living room? That bookcase is really dirty and none of the books are in order. They should be in order like at the library. Someone really should dust that bookcase and take care of those books. They're all over the room."

Kate stepped up to the kitchen sink and looked at the dishes but was careful not to touch them. She tried to make her voice as soothing and calm as possible. "The dishes look good. Very clean. I think-."

She stopped when she realized Mattie was no longer in the kitchen. She and September walked into the living room where Mattie was taking the rest of the paperbacks off the shelves and piling them on the floor according to color and size. She was muttering to herself about dust.

"Should I put the dishes away for you?" Mattie didn't even look up from her task.

"No, I'll do it." She looked at September, who had taken her hand off her mouth. "Don't talk to me. I don't want to hear you talk. Your voice hurts my ears."

September's eyes began to fill with tears as she nodded and put her hand back over her mouth. She didn't remember Lizzie ever being this bad and things with Lizzie had gotten worse than she'd ever admitted to anyone. Either Mattie had been using more than weed while she and Kate were dating and hid it well, or somehow Angel had gotten her into the hard stuff quickly. It had only been about a month since Angel and Mattie started dating.

Kate put an arm around her and led her back to her bedroom. "Why don't you go to bed?"

"Kate, I'm scared. I've never seen her like this." Kate hugged her. She knew exactly how September felt. She had never expected to see Mattie like this either.

"I'm a little scared myself. How about if I spend the night? I'll stay up and watch her till she crashes. I'll make sure she doesn't hurt herself."

September got Kate a blanket and a pillow for the couch and then crawled back into her bed, quickly falling into a restless sleep.

"September! You're back!" Lizzie jumped up from her bed and hugged September as she entered their dorm room. Surprised by the sudden display of affection after days of having been all but ignored by Lizzie, September slowly put her arms around Lizzie and hugged her back. "We're going out tonight and you can't say no. It's been too long since we've hung out."

"You're always with Brent. I never-." September broke off her complaint about Lizzie always being with Brent when she saw the flash of annoyance cross Lizzie's face. She had really missed spending time with Lizzie. "What do you want to do?"

"The Tri Sigs are having a party tonight and it's going to be off the chain!"

September sighed. Of course, she should have known. Brent was a Tri Sig so going to their party would mean he was there too. Lizzie would probably blow her off at some point, but she really didn't want to say no.

She and Lizzie had hardly talked lately. Maybe after the party they could hang out and eat cereal and talk like they used to. "Sure. Sounds good."

Lizzie must have sensed her hesitation. She grabbed September's arm. "I promise it will just be you and me. Just like old times."

September nodded. She wasn't sure she believed Lizzie, her promises never seemed to materialize any more, but she wanted to believe her. September smiled, hoping it looked more sincere than she felt. "It'll be great. What should we wear?"

"Oh! I have just the dress!" Lizzie pulled September across the room to their closets and pulled out a gauzy black babydoll dress and held it out. "Brent just bought me this. Isn't it cute?"

It's way too see through. September knew better than to say anything though. Lizzie was sensitive when it came to Brent's gifts. "Yeah, it's great."

She went to her own closet to look through her clothes. She planned on dressing for comfort. She pulled out a pair of jeans and a flowy green tank shirt. She threw them on her bed. She could wear them with her combat boots, and she would be comfortable and not look like she hadn't tried at all. Lizzie looked at what she had pulled out and frowned. "You can't wear that! You need to look hot! Brent's friend Dave thinks you're cute and he wants to talk to you tonight."

"Lizzie, I'm dating Tony." September frowned. How did Lizzie forget that? They still had a few hours till the party would start. It wasn't even quite dinner time and the party most likely wouldn't get underway until eight or nine. She watched, concerned, as Lizzie flitted around the room, seemingly unable to concentrate on any one thing long enough to complete it.

She sat on her bed and watched as Lizzie started to make herself a sandwich, then stopped to pull out her makeup caboodle and search through her lipsticks. Lizzie went over to their stereo, put in a cassette and danced around to the Book of Love song for a few minutes before returning to her sandwich.

Lizzie was acting strangely again. September wished she knew what was going on. This manic, unable to focus behavior wasn't like the Lizzie she knew at all. Lizzie's behavior had been getting more erratic the longer she was with Brent. She didn't think Brent was good for Lizzie and it wasn't just her jealousy over not getting to spend as much time with her best friend. At least, she didn't think it was. Something was up. Maybe she should talk to Spring about it. At the very least, maybe Spring's boyfriend, Mark, would know if the rumors about Brent being a drug dealer were true.

Chapter 13

September sighed as she unlocked the door and shoved her suitcase inside. She couldn't believe the highway was closed. She'd been looking forward to Thanksgiving with her family for weeks, and now she was going to have to spend it in Portales. She'd never spent Thanksgiving away from her family before and she really wished this wasn't the first one. She reached over and flipped on the light, rubbing her shoulder. The cold made her scar ache.

"Oh God! I'm sorry. I didn't know-."

September averted her eyes and bit her lip. Mattie and Angel were entangled on the floor, clad only in their panties. Mattie grabbed for her shirt, but Angel leaned back on her elbows, enjoying September's discomfort in her nudity.

"I thought you were going home for break."

"I tried. The snow closed the highway. I didn't realize you–had company."

"You can join us if you like." Angel smiled. Mattie nudged Angel to be quiet with an elbow.

"No. I'm going to–I'll see if Kate's home." September grabbed her suitcase and hurried out the door.

Please let Kate be home. I really don't want to spend Thanksgiving in the same house with those two going at it. Maybe she'll let me stay at her apartment while she goes home. God, I wish I could get home.

Kate answered the door and frowned when she saw September standing on her doorstep with her suitcase by her feet. "What are you doing here? I thought you'd be halfway to Oklahoma by now."

"Can I stay here over break? I-44 is closed, and the weatherman is predicting more snow tomorrow. I can't get home and Mattie and Angel are having sex on our living room floor."

"How do you know that?" Kate laughed.

"I walked in on them." September rolled her eyes.

"Gross." Kate picked up her own suitcase, which was sitting by the door, and nodded towards September's. "Grab your bag. The roads are clear up to Albuquerque. Come home with me."

"Your parents won't mind?"

"Not at all. Come on, I'm not letting you spend Thanksgiving by yourself. Get in the car."

The drive up to Albuquerque was pleasant. September and Kate discovered they both loved R.E.M. and ended up singing along to their newest CD at the top of their lungs, dissolving into laughter when they couldn't keep up with *It's the End of the World as We Know It.*

"She's here! She's here! Kate, you're home!" As soon as Kate pulled into the driveway, a five-year-old version of Kate in pigtails came running out the front door and launched herself into Kate's open arms.

"Munchkin, I missed you." Kate hugged the little girl tightly. "Give me a big kiss." She planted several loud kisses all over Kate's face.

"Melissa, don't run." A distinguished looking older man with graying blond hair and Kate's blue eyes and a younger blond woman in black slacks and a cream blouse walked out of the two story, impressive Spanish-style tan stucco house with a red tile roof.

"Hi, Twinkletoes. It's good to have you home, sweetheart." Kate's father kissed her cheek and gave her a hug, squeezing Melissa between them so she giggled. "We've got a lot planned for the next two days, don't we, Munchkin?"

"Doug, don't encourage them with those silly nicknames." The woman sighed. She noticed September standing on the other side of the car. "You didn't tell us you were bringing someone with you. We'll have to get another game hen for dinner."

"Please, don't. I'm a vegetarian."

Kate put Melissa down. She clung to Kate's hand. Kate waved September over with her free hand. "This is my friend, September. She couldn't get home for Thanksgiving, so I invited her here. This is my dad, Doug, his wife, Lindsey, and this munchkin here is my favorite sister in the entire world, Melissa."

Kate tickled her little sister as she introduced her. Melissa giggled and squirmed without really trying to get away.

"I'm your only sister!"

"Oh yeah." Kate tickled her again.

"It's nice to meet you, September. Welcome to our home." Doug shook September's hand.

"Thank you. I really appreciate this. I've never spent a holiday away from my family before."

Doug opened the door of Kate's VW Bug and pulled the girls' suitcases out of the car. "Let's get you inside and settled and then you can tell us about your trip."

"Are we still going to watch our movie since your friend is here?" Melissa was trying to walk backwards so she could look at Kate and still hold her hand. Kate scooped her up and swung her onto her back.

"Of course, we will. It's Thanksgiving, isn't it?"

"The guest room isn't made up since we didn't know you were coming." Lindsey led the way down the hallway.

"She can stay in my room with me." Kate pointed September to the room at the end of the hall. The room was painted in a soft shade of lavender with cream lace curtains and a queen-size four poster bed with matching bedspread and pillows. Georgia O'Keefe prints that matched the ones in her apartment hung on the walls and the blond wood dresser and armoire looked like antiques. The room was very feminine, and September was almost afraid to set foot on the plush carpet for fear she would mess up the room.

Kate had no such qualms. She threw her coat down on a chair, shut the door, and flopped down on the bed. "I can't believe Lindsey repainted my room again. Every time I come home it's different."

"Is she your-?"

"No. My parents divorced when I was thirteen. My dad remarried about a year later, and then I got my wonderful little munchkin."

"She is adorable. How do you and Lindsey get along?" September unzipped her bag and dug out a different sweater.

"Better now that I don't live here. She's okay, I guess."

"What movie do you two watch on Thanksgiving?"

"How do you feel about How the Grinch Stole Christmas?"

Chapter 14

September stood by the desk in Kate's father's study, phone to her ear.

"I've got to go, Dad. Dinner's ready. Tell Mom and Spring I love them." September nodded at Melissa to let the little girl know she'd heard her.

"Okay, Pumpkin. We'll talk to you tomorrow. Love you." Her dad was trying to sound cheerful, but September could hear how much he missed her.

"I love you too." September hung up the cordless phone and let Melissa lead her into the dining room. September slipped into the chair next to Kate's and put her linen napkin in her lap. The table was set much more formally than at September's house. There was a wine glass at every place, even though Melissa's was empty. There were too many forks and spoons lined up beside her plate. Even though she was wearing a skirt, Lindsey's look made her feel underdressed.

"Did you have a nice talk with your family?" Kate's father smiled as she sat down.

"Yes. Thank you again for having me. My parents were glad to hear I wasn't spending Thanksgiving by myself." September liked Kate's father. Watching him play with Melissa last night had reminded her of her father. Whether it was playing tea party with her dolls or taking her into his studio to help him paint the bookshelves he'd built for her, September's dad had always had time for her. She really missed her family.

"We're glad to have you." Doug smiled again.

September's own smile faltered when the server set a plate holding a game hen in front of her. September didn't mind other people eating meat in front of her, but the sight and smell of meat on her own plate made her sick to her stomach.

"Sara, before you leave for the day, will you please take September's plate away and bring her a clean one without the game hen?" Doug pointed to the offending plate as the gray-haired woman in black and white hurried to do as he asked.

Kate stared at Lindsey in disbelief. "Weren't you listening yesterday? She told you she didn't want one."

"It's Thanksgiving. I thought on a holiday like this, September would want the same meal as everyone else." Lindsey's blue eyes were widened with insincere regret.

"How come you don't want your chicken?" Melissa's eyes were bright with curiosity as she took in everything that was happening at the table.

"I'm a vegetarian." September took a roll from the basket Kate passed her and put it on her plate.

"What's that?" Melissa pressed her spoon into her mashed potatoes so her father could pour gravy on them.

"It means I don't eat meat."

"Not at all?" Melissa frowned at the asparagus her father put on her plate. "Not even in tacos?"

September laughed and shook her head. "Not even in tacos."

"What do your parents think about this? Wouldn't your mother be upset if you didn't eat her turkey?" Lindsey seemed determined to score some kind of point about September eating meat.

"My parents are vegetarians too. It's the way my sister and I were raised." September accepted more asparagus, but passed on the stuffing when Kate slightly shook her head no while passing it to her.

"Really?" Lindsey looked slightly disgusted, but Doug looked interested.

"Have you ever tried it?"

"Once." September rolled her eyes. What a mistake that had been. "I was probably thirteen. I was mad at my mom for something. I decided to get even with her by eating a cheeseburger in front of her. It didn't bother her at all, and I was sick for three days."

Everyone but Lindsey laughed. "What do you have on Thanksgiving?"

"Stuffed pumpkins."

Melissa giggled again. "Pumpkins are dessert!"

September smiled. "Not when they're stuffed with breadcrumbs and vegetables. We have apple pie for dessert."

"It sounds lovely. I'm sorry about the game hen, September. I honestly thought you would want it." Lindsey was saying the words, but September didn't believe she meant them.

"That's all right." September smiled at Lindsey. She wouldn't let Kate's stepmother bother her.

"So, what are you girls going to do after dinner?"

"We're going to go pick up our movie at the video store."

"Yay!" Melissa picked up her fork and ate the rest of her asparagus without complaint.

When they got back from the video store, Kate put the movies on top of her dresser. She and September had chosen some other movies to watch after Melissa's movie was finished.

Melissa crawled onto Kate's bed and flopped down against the pillows. Kate sat down beside her and put her arms around her little sister. "I'm sorry they didn't have our movie. We'll go back tomorrow and see if we can get it then, okay?"

Melissa leaned into her sister. "It's not the same."

Kate stroked Melissa's blond hair. "I know, Munchkin. I know, but it's the best I can do."

"Maybe not." September picked up the movie bag and brought it over to the bed. "Why don't you look in here and see what you can find?"

Kate glanced at September questioningly. Melissa sat up and dumped the bag out onto the bed. In the middle of the rental tapes, the bright green face of the Grinch stared up at her from a new copy of the movie they'd been unable to rent. Melissa grabbed it and hugged it to her. "Can I keep it?"

"Of course, you can. That's your very own copy so you never have to rent it again." September patted Melissa's knee. "How about if you put on your pajamas and then you and me and Kate will have a slumber party?"

Melissa looked at Kate. "Can we?"

"I'd love to have a slumber party with you. Go get changed and don't forget to brush your teeth." Melissa kissed Kate and September before running to change her clothes. Kate leaned over and hugged September. "You're the greatest. When did you get this?"

"While you were helping her pick out another movie. I had the guy at the counter sneak it into the bag."

"You put on your pajamas, and I'll go get snacks for our party." Kate headed into the kitchen.

September slipped into her flannel sleep bottoms and a baggy t-shirt. She unwrapped Melissa's movie and stacked it and the rentals on top of the television. September made a lounging area for them on the floor with pillows and blankets from the bed.

"What are you doing?" Melissa sat down between Kate and September and looked at the compartmentalized box full of beads in September's lap. She'd been getting small flashes of inspiration lately and was hoping to get some work done during the break.

"I'm making some barrettes. See?" September picked up the beaded barrette that she'd finished and handed it to Melissa.

"It's pretty."

"Thank you." September fastened the clip into Melissa's hair. "Why don't you keep them? They're not promised to anyone."

Kate examined the purple, pink, and white decoration in Melissa's hair. "I didn't know you did anything like this."

"It's been a while. I haven't felt like making any jewelry since Lizzie–since last year, but I'm starting to want to pick it up again." September picked up another bead with her needle.

"I'd love to see some other pieces." Kate got up to switch the tape. "You're going to love this movie, Munchkin. It was my favorite when I was little."

Melissa yawned as she curled up in Kate's lap to watch the movie. Kate stroked Melissa's hair as she giggled at the movie. Halfway through the film, she climbed up onto Kate's bed, pulling one of the pillows with her.

"Are you sure she's asleep? I can't believe we're watching this with her in the room." September glanced over her shoulder to the bed, where Melissa was curled up in a ball with her thumb in her mouth.

"I'm sure. I still can't believe you bought the video for her." Kate gave September a hug. "Thanks. She was so thrilled."

"She just looked so sad when they said it was checked out. Besides, if you rent it every year it's cheaper in the long run."

September had put her beadwork away, but she wasn't really paying attention to the scary movie they'd ended up renting. She was thinking about her phone call home earlier that day. Spring and Mark had announced their engagement and she'd missed it. She'd been looking forward to meeting Mark's parents. They had gone to dinner at the Ellis's house so the two families could meet. Now she probably wouldn't meet them until the wedding.

It was nice of Kate to bring her home with her and she was glad she wasn't spending the holiday alone, but Kate's stepmother made her uncomfortable. She felt like Lindsey was upset that she was in the house. Kate's dad was nice though. He and Melissa had both tried to make her feel at home.

"What're you thinking about?"

"I don't think Lindsey likes me."

"I think she thinks you're my girlfriend. She knows I'm a lesbian and it makes her uncomfortable. She doesn't know how to deal with it." Kate shrugged.

"But why would she think I'm your girlfriend?"

"She thinks every girl I bring home is my girlfriend. I'm sorry she's so rude. My dad and Melissa like you though." Kate shifted her position on the floor.

"I like them too. She is so cute. She absolutely worships you."

"I think that's part of Lindsey's problem." Kate grabbed the remote off the carpet beside her and quickly stopped the movie when she heard Melissa stir on the bed behind them. She got up and sat on the bed beside her sister. "Hey, Munchkin, what are you doing up?"

Chapter 15

"What's going on?" Kate asked September as they walked up the sidewalk to the house. The heavy repetitive bass of Nine-Inch Nails could be heard down the block. They were walking back from the coffee shop where they had been studying for their English classes. Midterms were coming up in less than a month.

"I don't know." September sighed and smoothed her hair back behind her ears. "Mattie and Angel must be having another party. I was hoping to get a break tonight. They've had parties every night this week. I've got a presentation tomorrow."

"I've got an extra bedroom at my place."

"Thanks." Stepping past the small group of people smoking on the porch, September opened the door and let Kate and herself in. The air was thick with cigarette smoke and the smell of marijuana. About fifteen people were sitting around the living room listening to music and passing around a joint. A small group in the corner was hunched over an end table. Beer cans littered the coffee table and floor. A girl September recognized from past parties at the house was passed out on the couch. A few couples were making out on the floor. September saw Angel sitting on the floor watching the television with the sound turned off with another girl. She didn't see Mattie anywhere. She and Kate picked their way through the beer cans into September's room. Shutting the door did nothing to soften the level of the music. September felt a headache quickly building.

"Is it always like this?"

"Yes. It's been getting worse lately. I don't know what to do, Kate." September sat down on the bed and hugged a slightly tattered dog to her chest.

"You've got to talk to her." Kate sat down beside her.

"I know, but what do I say? Angel is her girlfriend. I'm sure she's getting the drugs from Angel, but bad-mouthing her girlfriend isn't exactly going to want to make her do what I'm asking her to do."

"True, but you don't have to bring up Angel at all. Just tell her the truth. You're worried about her and think she's getting in over her head. Tell her if she doesn't stop, you're going to move out."

September sighed. "I know you're right. I do need to talk to her." September yawned. "I haven't had a decent night's sleep all week."

"Come on, I'll go with you to ask her to break up the party. If it doesn't work, you can come stay with me." Kate put her hand on September's shoulder.

"It won't work, Kate. She won't break up the party till she wants to." September shook her head sadly.

"Well, we can ask anyway. You need some sleep. Maybe she'll do it if she knows you have a presentation tomorrow." September sighed and stood up, following Kate out of her bedroom and into the living room.

Mattie was sitting on the couch, slowly sipping a rum and coke, and staring off into space. September and Kate stood in front of her for a few minutes before she noticed them. "Hey, want a drink?" She held up her glass. September and Kate could smell the alcohol on her breath.

"No. Can I talk to you?" September nodded towards Mattie's bedroom.

"Okay, sure. What's up?" Mattie stood up and walked unsteadily to her bedroom. She almost tripped on a beer can. September and Kate followed.

"Mattie, I have to give a presentation tomorrow morning. You've been having parties all week. I really need some sleep. Do you think you could break up the party or turn the music down?" September sat down on Mattie's bed and fought a yawn. Mattie dug around on her dresser top until she found a bottle. She opened it and offered its contents to September.

"Here, take this. It'll put you to sleep. You won't even notice the party, I promise." Kate looked at September and shut the door to Mattie's bedroom. September clenched her hands into fists and forced herself to unclench them. She knocked the pill bottle out of Mattie's hand.

"Hey!" Mattie dropped to her knees, drink still in hand, and started scrambling to pick up the pills.

"Do you see what you're doing?" September grabbed Mattie's drink from her and pulled on her arm. "You're offering me drugs to sleep so you can keep the drug den in the living room going. Do you get how fucked up that is?"

Mattie stood up and tried to grab her drink back from September but missed. "Give that back! That's my drink!" Mattie tried to grab it again.

"No." September took a deep breath to try and calm down. "Mattie, I want you to listen to me. You're so drunk and stoned I doubt you'll hear any of it, but I–." September stopped as Mattie lunged at her. September sidestepped her and threw the contents of the glass in Mattie's face when Mattie turned to come at her again.

"You bitch!" Mattie came towards September but froze when she grabbed the pill bottle off the dresser where Mattie had set it and rushed into the bathroom Mattie had turned into a darkroom. She lifted the lid to the toilet and held the bottle over it.

"Stay where you are, Mattie." Mattie's eyes were glued to the bottle in September's hand. She was shaking.

Kate stepped in and took the bottle from September. "This isn't getting us anywhere."

As soon as Kate had taken the bottle from September, Matie charged towards her again. She hit September across the face and shoved her into the wall. Kate stepped in, grabbed Mattie by her shoulders and shook her. "Mattie, what the fuck are you doing?"

September sat on the floor for a moment, stunned. She got to her feet and went into Mattie's bedroom. Mattie stopped struggling so Kate let go of her. As soon as Kate had released her, Mattie ran after September and tackled her from behind. She knocked her to the floor and punched her. September threw up her hands to try and protect herself. Kate pulled Mattie off her and held her against the wall. Kate was small, but she was strong. September sat on the bed, pinching the bridge of her nose to stop the bleeding.

Mattie stopped struggling as she realized what she'd done and the two of them saw a tear run down September's cheek. She couldn't believe Mattie had hit her. Her nose and cheek hurt from where she'd hit them on the floor. Mattie broke away from Kate and knelt on the floor in front of September. Mattie touched September's arm. She flinched and pulled away. "September, I'm so sorry! I didn't mean to hurt you!"

"Mattie. I'm worried about you." September took the tissue Kate offered her and wiped her nose with it.

"Worried about me? Why?" Mattie looked puzzled.

"Why? Mattie, you're drunk almost every night, you're high whenever you're awake, and you never go to class anymore! You're poisoning yourself." September dropped a hand into Mattie's hair.

"No, I'm not. I'm opening my mind to new possibilities. Getting high helps my creative processes; I can come up with incredible new ideas. It's opening all sorts of new doors for my work." Mattie pulled back to look at September. She couldn't understand why she was so worried. She was doing great.

"Mattie, you haven't done any new work since those pictures you took of me. That was two months ago. Where is all this new incredible work you're able to do? That opening your mind stuff is bullshit and you know it!"

"No, it's not! Just because I haven't shot any of my ideas doesn't mean I haven't had them."

"Mattie, you're killing your creativity. You're killing yourself." September was determined to try and make Mattie see her side. She knew if Mattie was thinking clearly, she would be appalled at where her photography was headed.

"No, September, I'm not. I wish you could see that. Angel told me you wouldn't understand. I was hoping you would."

"Mattie, you hit me. I thought your work was about celebrating women. What kind of celebration is that? I don't think that's the kind of inspiration you want." September sighed. Kate stood silently to the side. She was ready to jump in again if September needed her, but she didn't think Mattie would listen to her, so she kept quiet.

"September, I'm sorry I hit you. I didn't mean to." Mattie put her arms around September's waist and put her head in her lap. Hesitantly, September stroked Mattie's hair. Tears filled her eyes again.

"I know you didn't mean it, but you did it."

"I won't do it again. I promise." Mattie lifted her head. "Please don't cry. I swear I'll never hit you again." She suddenly seemed much more sober than she had when the conversation started.

"Mattie," September sighed. "I believe you mean it, but I don't believe you can keep that promise. I can't live like this. I'm not sleeping. I'm afraid of the people in my house, I'm afraid of you."

"Of me? September, you don't need to be afraid of me! I'll never touch you again, I swear!" Mattie clutched at September's hand, desperate to make her believe her.

"As long as you're taking drugs, you might." September took a deep breath. You're doing this for her, September told herself. If you care about her, you have to try to get her off drugs. "Mattie, I don't know who you are most of the time anymore. I care too much about you to watch you do this to yourself. I can't do this anymore."

"Can't do what?"

"If you don't stop drinking so much, if you don't stop taking all the drugs and having parties all the time, I'm going to move out."

September took a deep breath and stood up. Mattie stayed on the floor. Mattie looked at her hands for a few moments and then up at September.

"I don't want you to move out."

"Then this has to stop. I mean it, Mattie. I don't want to keep coming home to all these people doing drugs in my house. I don't want to come home to find you passed out in the living room. I want things back to the way they were. I can't watch you do this to yourself. Not after Lizzie. If things don't change, I'm moving out at the end of the month."

"September, I swear I'll change! Please don't move out. I want you to stay."

"Stop the drinking and the drugs and start going to class again. If things get better, I'll stay. If things don't get better, I'll move out at the end of the month. If you hit me again, I'll move out immediately."

"I promise. I'll do whatever you want, just don't leave." Mattie stood up and hugged September. September reluctantly hugged her back and then pulled away and followed Kate out of the bedroom.

"Hey, you're shaking." Kate put an arm around September.

"I wish I believed her." September yawned. She winced as her face twinged in pain. "I'm going to go grab my things for tomorrow. I'll be back in a minute."

September ran a hand through her hair and sighed as she shut her bedroom door behind her. It did nothing to diminish the pounding of the stereo or her head. Thank God Kate was going to let her stay at her apartment tonight. She didn't think she could take another night of the loud, pulsating music, smoke and noise that accompanied Mattie's parties. September definitely did not want to wake up again to find another drugged-out couple trying to sneak into her bed to have sex.

She left the overhead light off and flipped on the lamp beside her bed. Maybe the dim light would help ease her headache. September turned toward the closet to get her overnight bag and jumped. Angel was leaning against the wall, watching her. Her eyes were feverishly bright. She was wearing her standard black leather miniskirt.

"Hello, September." Angel smiled lazily; her eyes moved over September's body in a way that gave her the creeps.

"What're you doing in here?" September grabbed her bag and the clothes she wanted from the closet and carried them over to the bed. September had decided the best course of action with Angel was to ignore her whenever possible and pretend she didn't bother her the rest of the time.

"I thought we should have a little chat." September kept her back to Angel. She felt Angel standing behind her before she heard her move. Angel lightly raked her nails up September's bare arms.

"We don't have anything to talk about." September stopped packing and stood still as Angel wrapped one arm around September's waist, pinning her arm to her side. Angel's grip was surprisingly strong.

"I think we do." Angel's other hand continued to run up and down September's arm. "For a girl with a boyfriend, you're awfully curious about what Mattie and I do."

"I don't know what you mean." September wished she felt as brave as she was trying to sound.

"I've seen you watching us. Watching Mattie. I know you want her." Angel's breath was hot against September's neck as Angel whispered in her ear.

"Don't be ridiculous. I have Tony. Why would I want Mattie?" September hoped Angel bought her bravado. She had been watching Mattie and Angel. Reading Mattie's lesbian books wasn't the same as seeing two women together.

"I know you have Tony. I also know he doesn't do a thing for you." Angel's hand around her waist had worked its way under September's gray top and was stroking her stomach.

September bit her lip. She was glad Angel couldn't see her face. "You're wrong. I love him."

"Am I? I heard you two having sex. I know you were faking." The hand that had been running up and down her arm was now sliding down the side of September's skirt.

How did Angel know? How could she tell? The questions raced through September's head before she registered what they meant. "You were listening to us? That's disgusting! I–."

"I notice you're not denying it." Angel's hand under her shirt inched its way up to her ribs.

"Stop that." September wanted to move. Her brain was screaming at her to break away from Angel, but something was holding her to the spot. She couldn't move.

Angel suddenly reminded her of the evil octopus in the kid's movie about the mermaid. She seemed to be wrapped around September, everywhere at once. Angel's breasts and hip bones were pressed against September's back. The hand around her waist had inched its way high enough that if Angel tilted her hand, she would be cupping September's breast in her palm.

"You faked it because he can't get you all hot and bothered, can he?"

"Yes, he does." September's voice was only a whisper. Her breathing quickened as she felt Angel's hand on her leg begin slowly moving upwards, pulling her skirt with it. September made a feeble attempt to push Angel's hands away, but she was pinned. "Don't. I don't want you to do that."

"What about Mattie? Would you like Mattie to do this to you?" Angel kissed her neck. Angel's voice seemed to be coming in both ears at once. September felt like she was drowning.

"She will if I ask her. She likes threesomes when she's rolling." Angel licked September's ear and tried to nibble on her earlobe. September turned her head away.

"Mattie could make you wet like Tony never could. I can tell you exactly what she'd do to you." Angel paused. "Of course, maybe you're wet already."

The feel of Angel's fingers trying to slip underneath the elastic of September's panties snapped her out of her frozen state. She pushed Angel away from her and slapped her across the face.

"Don't ever touch me like that!" September forced herself not to take a step back when Angel stepped towards her.

Angel stood inches away from September. She ran her fingers through a piece of September's long, red hair and smiled. "Mattie's mine. If you want her, and I know you do, You'll have to sleep with both of us."

"I don't want either of you. I have Tony."

"Just keep telling yourself that."

Before September could answer, Kate opened the door to September's bedroom. "Are you ready?"

Kate looked from Angel to September in confusion as Angel let go of September's hair and kissed her cheek, leaving a dark red lipstick mark.

"Don't worry, September. I'll make sure you know just how wet a woman can make you."

"Get out of here, Angel." Kate shoved Angel out the door.

September's legs suddenly turned to rubber. She sank down onto the bed. She didn't know which bothered her more, that she had let Angel touch her that intimately, or that the thought of Mattie touching her like that made her more excited than the thought of having sex with Tony did. She jumped when Kate sat down beside her and put an arm around her shoulders.

"Are you okay?" Kate looked at September's untucked shirt and wrinkled skirt. "What happened? She didn't try to force you into anything, did she?"

September shook her head. She couldn't tell Kate what had happened. All she wanted was to get into a bathtub for a long soak. Her skin crawled where Angel had touched her. "No. She just—if she's telling the truth, Mattie's doing more than just speed."

Kate sighed and gave September a squeeze. She stood up and picked up September's bag. "Come on, let's get you out of here. Whatever isn't packed you can borrow."

Chapter 16

September's phone rang for what seemed like the hundredth time that day. She knew it was Spring, or her mom, or some other well-meaning person from home, so she let the answering machine get it again. September didn't feel like talking to anyone. She'd skipped classes and hadn't even bothered to change out of her pajamas. The only thing she had done was work on the sculpture she'd promised Lizzie's parents. She was about to tear it down and start over for the fifth time. Nothing she did seemed right. She'd thought she knew Lizzie better than anybody. The realization that she hadn't was making it difficult to capture her essence.

"Come on, we're going out tonight." Mattie walked into September's room, opened her closet door, and began rummaging through her clothes. September stared at Mattie in amazement for a few minutes before standing up.

"Mattie, I appreciate the invite, but I don't really feel like it. Maybe some other time."

Today should have been Lizzie's twenty-first birthday. They'd been planning this day since they were sixteen and now, they'd never get to have their celebration. September just wanted to stay home and feel sorry for herself.

"Nope, you're not getting out of it. When you wouldn't answer your phone, Spring called me. I know what today is. You should've told me. I'm not letting you sit here in the dark. We're going out and we're celebrating Lizzie's birthday so put these on and be ready to go in an hour." Mattie threw the black pleather pants September had bought in a momentary fit of insanity and a green low-cut tank top she'd selected from September's closet and threw them on the bed. One look at Mattie's face told her there was no changing her mind. September put the tank top back in her closet. It would show too much of her scar. She pulled out a blue top that reminded her of a bikini top with sleeves and added it to the pants.

Mattie whistled when September came out of the bathroom. "You look great. I love that necklace. Where did you get it?"

September fingered the beaded choker around her neck. "I made it."

"You have got to make me a necklace. I love your stuff."

"It's been a while since I designed anything new, but maybe for Christmas."

Mattie grabbed September's hand. "Come on, it's time to put a smile on your face and have some fun."

"Mattie, where are we?" September whispered in Mattie's ear as they entered the dark club. It had taken an hour and a half to get there and now, everywhere September looked, women were dancing with each other, kissing, and talking animatedly in large groups. She'd never been anywhere like it.

"Triangles. It's a lesbian bar. I thought you'd enjoy it. It's one of the few clubs that has really good dance music and people let you dance without hitting on you if you don't act interested." Mattie grabbed September's hand and pulled her out onto the crowded dance floor. "Come on, you'll have fun."

September started dancing with Mattie. They were playing one of her favorite songs. The club was dark enough that September could indulge her curiosity and watch the women together as long as she didn't stare for too long. She'd felt too uncomfortable and obvious watching Mattie and Kate, but she could watch the women here to her heart's content without worrying about what anyone thought.

A woman near the bar caught her eye. She was wearing a tuxedo jacket over a filmy shirt she had left unbuttoned all the way down. She wasn't wearing a bra. September couldn't help herself. She watched the woman, expecting to see her shirt fly open at any moment. Mattie finally realized September wasn't paying attention to her. She glanced over her shoulder and smiled. "Spicy. I hope she doesn't plan on dancing later."

"I would never have enough courage to do that." September shook her head and fanned herself.

"Go grab that table. I'm going to get us something to drink." Mattie pointed to an empty table along the wall. September fanned herself again, nodded, and sat down at the table. She looked around her and noticed the framed pictures on the walls for the first time. Portraits of k.d. lang, Marilyn Monroe, Ellen, and other women September supposed must be lesbian icons adorned the walls. There were two television monitors in the corners.

September gasped as she looked at them and saw two naked women embracing. What must have been a tape of some kind continued, with a variety of images of women in various embraces and sexual situations flashing across the screen. She stared, unable to tear her eyes away until a woman who looked familiar sat down across from her.

"Hi. I don't know if you remember me, but we met at one of Mattie's parties. I'm Heather." September nodded. She was speechless. The woman with the unbuttoned shirt had sat down across from her. Now that she was closer, September recognized her.

"You were with the girl wearing that great black lace dress, right?"

"Yes." Heather smiled. Her short dark hair was slicked back from her face. She ran a hand over it as she leaned forward towards September. The shirt gaped a little but stayed in place. "I haven't seen you here before. A lot of people from Mattie's parties hang out here."

"This is my first time. Mattie brought me."

"Oh." Heather sat back a little. "Are you and she together now?"

"Together?"

"Well, I know she and Kate were fighting about you moving in. I thought maybe you two were dating now."

"Oh, no. Mattie's just my friend." September glanced towards the bar. It was taking Mattie a long time to get their drinks. Heather saw her glance and mistook it as a glance towards the dance floor.

"Do you want to dance?" September hesitated and then nodded. It was just a dance and Heather was one of Mattie's friends. She hoped Heather's shirt didn't come open. Heather left her drink sitting on the table and they went back out to the dance floor. The dance started out fine. It was a great song and Heather was a good dancer. As they continued to dance though, Heather kept getting closer and closer to September. She kept backing up until she was blocked in on all sides by dancers. The song changed and suddenly Heather was pressed up against September, grinding her hips into September's and grabbing her around the waist to pull her even closer. September put her hands on Heather's shoulders and tried to push her away right as Heather leaned in and tried to kiss her.

September stepped backwards, tripping over the foot of the woman behind her and falling. The woman caught her and helped her up as Mattie pushed Heather back.

"I'm sorry. Are you okay?" September's face was the same color as her hair as she apologized to the woman she'd stumbled over. The woman nodded and she turned toward Heather. "What the hell was that? Couldn't you tell I didn't want you that close to me?"

"I'm sorry. You said you and Mattie weren't dating and I thought you were staring at me earlier. I guess I was mistaken." Heather touched September's arm. "Give me another chance. I won't get that close again. I promise."

"No, I think I've had enough dancing for now. I'm going to sit down." September walked back to their table and sat down. Mattie gave Heather a warning look when she started to follow and joined September.

"Are you okay? What happened? I was coming back with drinks, and I saw you fall."

"She was all over me! I was trying to get away from her, and I tripped." September took a big drink of the water Mattie handed her.

"I'm sorry. Heather's nice, but she can be kind of aggressive sometimes. She's been asking about you since the party. I told her you have a boyfriend, but she likes to try and hook up with straight girls." Mattie glanced over her shoulder to see what September was staring at. She smiled. "Pretty spicy stuff, huh? If she saw you staring at the screen like that, no wonder she made a move on you."

September tore her eyes away from the screen and blushed again. Mattie was right. The women on the screen were sexy. She sat staring at her drink, not knowing what to say. The lights dimmed even more, and the DJ put on a slow song.

Mattie held out her hand. "Dance with me."

September shook her head. She couldn't imagine going back out on the dance floor and standing that close to Mattie in front of everyone. "I don't think so."

"Come on. Dance with me and no one will bother you anymore. They'll think you're here with me." Mattie smiled. September felt herself give in just like she always had when Lizzie smiled at her.

"Okay." September let Mattie lead her onto the dance floor. After a moment's hesitation, she let Mattie pull her close and laid her head on Mattie's shoulder. Mattie's arms around her felt good. September began to relax. She saw something move out of the corner of her eye and turned her head slightly. The woman was pointing at September.

Mattie must have felt her stiffen, because she tilted her head slightly and whispered, "What's wrong?"

"Those two women are talking about me."

"I'm sure they're not." Mattie whispered. She moved September around the dance floor. They ended up near the two women.

"She's such a slut. Did you see the way she was dancing with Heather and then she didn't want her anywhere near her when her girlfriend showed up. Women like her make me sick."

September heard them and froze in Mattie's arms. Mattie had heard them too. She gave September a squeeze. September was fighting back tears. She pulled back slightly and looked at Mattie. "Can we go home now?"

Mattie looked at September silently for a moment before nodding.

Chapter 17

A small scratching noise invaded September's sleep. She let out a soft sigh and rolled over. She heard the sound again. September threw an arm over her ear to block out the sound. A pounding on the living room window made September sit up and pay attention. She heard it again. She knew she was alone in the house. September listened for a few more minutes. Her heart was pounding. She grabbed the cordless phone and hid in her closet.

"9-1-1. What's your emergency?" The woman on the other end of the phone was all business. Just hearing someone else's voice was comforting.

"I think someone's trying to break into my house. I keep hearing something at the living room windows." September wanted to get out of the closet and turn on the lights, but fear kept her pinned in place. That might scare them away, but it might make them attack her.

"What do you hear?"

"At first, it was just a small sound, but now it's louder, like pounding, like they're trying to break the glass." She could still hear the noises. They were getting more insistent. Her heart was pounding faster, it was getting hard to breathe. She wanted this woman to stop asking her questions and tell her someone was on the way.

"Are you sure it's not just a tree or a pet?"

September tried to control the annoyance in her voice, she couldn't stop the trembling. "We don't have any pets and there aren't any trees on that side of the house."

"What's your address?'

"Four-oh-five Avenue J."

"Okay, I've alerted the police and they're on their way. I need you to stay inside and lock the door if possible."

September knew the door was locked. Ever since Mattie started dating Angel, September always kept the door locked. She stayed in the closet, shaking and trying to control her breathing, until she heard car doors slamming and men's voices shouting at someone to get down. She hesitantly opened the closet door. Red and blue lights flashed against her curtains. *Shit!* She recognized the voice that answered them, tossed the phone onto her bed, and ran towards the front door.

The scene was surreal enough without the flashing lights from the police car. Memories from last year mixed in with the actual scene in front of September, making her dizzy. She should have known. Mattie was face down on the ground, struggling against the two police officers who were holding her down. She was screaming at the top of her lungs. "What the fuck are you doing? Let me go! I live here! Let me go!"

September stood on the porch for a moment, trying to stop the feeling that everything was spinning, before she found her voice. "She's right. She does live here." September turned her attention to Mattie. "What were you doing? You scared the shit out of me! Why didn't you ring the doorbell?"

The police helped Mattie stand up. She tried to shrug them off, but she was having trouble keeping her balance. "I lost my keys. I didn't want to wake you up." Mattie's words were slightly slurred. One of the police officers took her arm and led her over to the car.

September watched as he ran Mattie through various sobriety tests. She failed them all. She hurried down the steps as the officer handcuffed Mattie and began putting her in the back of his car. Mattie began fighting him with all her strength. She was screaming, kicking, and trying to bite. It took both of the officers to get her into the car. "What are you doing?"

"I'm taking her in. She tried to flee and backed into our car when we got here. She's obviously under the influence and now she's assaulted a police officer."

"How did she drive if she lost her keys? Do you have to? She's home now. I wouldn't have called if I'd known she lost her keys. Please."

"Sorry, miss. You can come to the police station and bail her out if you want to, but I have to take her in. She's so drunk she didn't realize she left her keys in the ignition." The police officer told her where to go at the station to post bail. The neighbors who had come outside to see what the commotion was about, began to go back inside.

September watched the police car pull away. She closed her eyes and sighed. What a night. The outcome was better than last year, September reminded herself. She wasn't hurt and Mattie was alive. She couldn't believe Mattie had tried to break into the house instead of just ringing the doorbell. Now that the excitement was over, September realized she was cold. She looked down and realized she hadn't put on her robe before running into the yard. She wrapped her arms around herself and went into the house.

She searched her bed until she found the phone and dialed from memory. "Kate, Mattie's been arrested. I need to go bail her out, but I–I don't think I can drive right now. Can you come?"

The bail process took longer than the police officer had made it sound like it would. Kate and September were exhausted, and to make matters worse, Mattie had thrown up in the car on the way back to the house.

"I still say you should've let her spend the night in the drunk tank. Maybe she would've learned a lesson." Kate grunted as she lifted the water bucket out of her backseat and dumped the dirty, soapy water onto the asphalt. She jumped back as water splashed her shoes.

"You know it would be worse if I'd left her there all night." September handed Kate her rag and then awkwardly climbed out of the VW bug's backseat. She sprayed the upholstery with fabric deodorizer one more time before she shut the door. "Make sure you didn't leave anything valuable in your car. I think you ought to leave the windows down tonight."

"At least she wouldn't have puked in my car." Kate threw the rags into the bucket and headed towards September's front porch. "I will. Thanks for helping me clean it up. It would've reeked tomorrow."

"God, I hope she's passed out." September had a headache. Mattie had been alternately belligerent and thankful about Kate and September bailing her out. It had cost September next month's rent to get her out and she doubted Mattie was going to care where the money had gone when the rent was due.

Mattie was not passed out. She saw them come in and staggered up from the couch. September stiffened as Mattie came towards them.

"You! You should've told the police I–." Mattie slurred her words and stumbled as she reached them. She grabbed September for support and threw up all over September's shoulder. September swallowed against the bile rising in her own throat at the warm, disgusting liquid running down her shoulder, and struggled for balance as Mattie put her full weight on her and tried to stand up straight. Kate grabbed one of Mattie's arms and helped her.

"Come on, Mattie. Let's get you into the bathroom." They were almost there when Mattie groaned, shoved them away, and lurched towards the toilet.

"Ow!" Mattie had shoved September into the doorframe before she could catch herself. September grabbed her shoulder.

"Go sit on your bed. I'll be right there." Kate turned her and gently pushed her towards her bedroom.

"But–." September gestured towards Mattie.

"She's not going anywhere. Let's get you cleaned up and put some ice on that." Kate gave September a small push towards her room, "Go, sit."

September sat down on the edge of her bed and wrinkled her nose at the smell coming from her shirt. She felt disgusting, her shoulder hurt, and she was exhausted. Kate appeared beside her and handed her an ice pack. "Hold this."

Kate knelt down in front of her and picked up a washcloth out of a bowl of warm, soapy water. She started cleaning September's shoulder.

"I can do that."

"You just hold that ice."

September watched as Kate rinsed out the washcloth and began wiping off her shoulder again. She held her breath as Kate cleaned her shirt right over her scar. She watched Kate's hands, fascinated with how graceful her every movement was. Kate's choice of baby blue nail polish always surprised her. Kate took the ice away from her. September snapped out of her reverie as she realized Kate was untucking her shirt.

"What are you doing?"

Kate rolled her eyes. "Relax. I'm just going to help you get this off without getting vomit in your hair. I'm not going to look."

Slowly, Kate helped September get the shirt off without getting anything on her face or hair. True to her word, Kate averted her eyes while September changed into her pajamas.

"Do you want to crash here?"

"I'd love to. I am wiped." Kate flipped off the overhead light and slipped into the bed beside September.

September leaned against the wall, her first plastic cup of beer still in her hand. She didn't feel like drinking, but if she held it instead of a soda, which was what she really wanted, the frat boys didn't come up to her constantly asking her if they could get her a drink. She shrank against the wall as a group of drunken girls pushed by her, stumbling and giggling, trying to get into the room where several of the fraternity boys were playing beer pong and doing keg stands. September glanced at her watch and sighed. Ten o'clock. Less than two hours since they'd arrived and Lizzie had already ditched her after trying to hook her up with Dave, despite her reminder that she was still dating Tony.

September looked around the crowded room, trying to catch a glimpse of Lizzie. This was ridiculous! She didn't want to be here. She hated frat parties and Lizzie knew it. The only reason she had come tonight was because Lizzie had said she wanted to spend time together and had promised not to ditch her. She knew she had to stand up for herself. She couldn't let Lizzie treat her this way. She was giving Lizzie ten more minutes and if she hadn't come back by then, she was going to find her and tell Lizzie she was leaving and if she wanted to stay, Brent could give her a ride home.

She felt the beginnings of tears prickling in the corners of her eyes and tried to force them back. She would not cry at the frat party. She would wait until she got back to their dorm room and then she could cry all she wanted to. She was losing Lizzie and she didn't know how or why or if there was anything she could do to fix it. She wished Lizzie had never started working at Spencers. She never would have met Brent if she hadn't been working there. September checked her watch again. She had let herself wallow longer than she thought. Her watch read almost ten-thirty. She pushed off the wall and went in search of Lizzie.

September had made her way around the entire first floor twice and hadn't found Lizzie or Brent. She'd disposed of her cup of beer too early in her haste to find Lizzie and get out of there and now she was hampered every few minutes by another guy trying to get her a drink. Out of desperation, she finally talked to one of them wearing a Tri Sig shirt instead of brushing him off.

"Do you know where Brent is and if Lizzie is with him?"

"I think I saw them head upstairs a little while ago." He looked September up and down and smiled what she was sure he thought was a charming smile. "Do you want to go upstairs?"

"Not with you. I just need to find Lizzie and tell her I'm leaving."

Now that September had blown him off, he was less helpful. "His room is the third door on the right on the second floor. Good luck." His smile was different now, more sinister somehow. September brushed him off and pushed her way through the throngs of drunk co-eds and frat boys to the stairs. She ducked under the caution tape used to block them off and went to the second-floor landing. The guy she had talked to hadn't been helpful enough to tell her if his room was to the left of the landing or the right. She heard what sounded like a moan coming from the right and went in that direction praying they were at least under the covers. She paused at what she hoped was the right door and knocked.

"Lizzie? Lizzie, are you in there?"

Brent opened the door, naked from the waist up. His eyes were red and bloodshot. "Who are you?"

"Her roommate, remember? We've met before." September curled her lip at the scent of pot wafting from the room. "I'm leaving. I wanted to tell her she's going to need to find another ride home if she's staying."

Brent opened the door wide. "Nah, you can take her home. She's too wasted to be any fun tonight." He opened the door and September could see Lizzie slumped in a chair, head on Brent's desk.

"What the fuck happened to her?" September rushed in and shook Lizzie, trying to rouse her.

"She can't hold her alcohol." Brent laughed. "Get her out of here. I'm going to find a girl who can party as hard as I can."

"God, you're an asshole." September somehow managed to get Lizzie to her feet, put an arm around Lizzie's waist and looped one of Lizzie's arms around her shoulders, standing her up. She struggled to hold up Lizzie's weight. "Come on Lizzie. I need you to walk."

September struggled with getting Lizzie into the car. Fortunately, Lizzie had waited to completely pass out until they were almost to the car, but now September was struggling with what was essentially dead weight trying to get Lizzie into the passenger seat. The gauzy babydoll dress Lizzie had chosen to wear kept getting in her way as she tried to buckle Lizzie into the seat while trying to keep her from slumping over.

"Fuck it! It's not far." September finally gave up trying to buckle Lizzie in and just reclined the seat, so Lizzie didn't keep falling forward. She stood up, breathing hard after all the effort of getting Lizzie to the car and into the seat. "Fucking Brent, you'd better dump his ass after this." September vented, walking around to get into the driver's seat. Driving *the back roads might take a little longer, but there wouldn't be as much traffic. "You and I are going to have breakfast and a serious talk tomorrow morning." She muttered to an unconscious Lizzie as she pulled away from the frat house.*

Carefully, September maneuvered them down the back roads towards their dorm, singing along with the radio in a half-hearted attempt to calm herself down. She was angry with Lizzie for breaking her promise and ditching her at the party, she was angry with herself for believing Lizzie yet again, and she was angry with Brent for tossing Lizzie aside and leaving her for September to take care of. She was concentrating so hard on the lyrics of the song; she was startled when Lizzie suddenly jerked herself up and awake.

"What? Where are we?"

"We're headed home." September glanced over at Lizzie. "Now that you're awake, will you-?"

"No! What the hell? Why did you make me go home?" Lizzie swatted at September.

"Stop! I didn't make you go home, Brent told me to take you home. You were out of it." September flinched as Lizzie swatted at her again.

"No! He wouldn't do that! Take me back!"

"He told me to take you home," September took a deep breath. "He told me he was going to find another girl who could keep up with him." She glanced over at Lizzie. "I'm sorry."

"Liar!" Lizzie leaned in and started hitting September. "He wouldn't say that! You're just jealous. You pulled me out of there! Take me back!"

"Stop!" September tried to ward off Lizzie's blows and keep her hands on the wheel.

"Take me back!" Lizzie grabbed the wheel and jerked it hard towards her.

"Lizzie, stop! Stop!" September screamed as the car jerked onto the shoulder. "You're going to make us crash, let go!"

"September, September, wake up!" September jerked awake, not quite sure for a split second where she was or who was shaking her. She stared blankly at Kate before her brain kicked in and she could process the information around her.

"Kate?" September rubbed her eyes.

"You were talking in your sleep. Are you okay?" Kate studied her face.

"Yeah, I-I'm sorry I woke you. Go back to sleep." September rolled over and tried to will herself to think of something else.

Chapter 18

"Another party?" It had only been a couple of days since they had bailed Mattie out of jail. Kate looked at September with raised eyebrows as they walked up the cracked sidewalk to September's house. The bulb in the front porch light had been changed to a black light. The purplish light highlighted the small white patches in the house's stucco finish. A guy sitting on the porch steps was smoking a cigarette and talking to a girl in a black minidress.

"She asked this time. It's Gena's birthday." September opened the screen door and let Kate walk in ahead of her.

Compared to the parties Mattie had been throwing, this one was small. There were about twenty-five people scattered around the dimly lit living room and kitchen. The furniture had been pushed back against the walls to make room for people to dance and Mattie had hung a large piece of paper and a marker on the wall for people to write Heather well wishes on. September noticed someone had missed the paper completely and hoped it wasn't a permanent marker.

An old Garbage CD was playing on the stereo and the television was tuned to MTV with the sound off. Two couples were dancing in the middle of the living room while another couple was making out on the couch. Almost everyone was drinking, but no one seemed to be doing any drugs. The only smoke in the air September could smell was definitely cigarette smoke.

When Kate and September's eyes had adjusted to the dim light, they found Mattie and Angel coming out of the kitchen. Mattie was wearing her usual jeans and a black lace-edged tank top under a sheer shirt. Angel was wearing a black leather mini skirt and bustier. Mattie offered them a bite of the chocolate chip cookie she was eating.

"I thought you were allergic to nuts." September looked at Mattie questioningly.

"What made you think that?"

September shook her head as if to clear it. *That was Lizzie.* "I—nothing."

"Let me get you some of my special brew." Angel went back into the kitchen and returned a few minutes later with two large cups of red liquid with fruit floating in them. She handed them to September and Kate.

September looked at the cup suspiciously and sniffed at the contents. It looked and smelled like Kool-Aid. Kate seemed familiar with the drink. She pulled a cherry out of the glass, ate it, and took a sip of the drink.

"What is it?" September continued to eye the cup. She didn't trust anything Angel gave her.

"It's a peace offering. If you're Mattie's friend, I want us to be friends too." Angel smiled sweetly.

"It's jungle juice." Mattie raised her own glass and took a drink. "Try it."

"It tastes like fruit punch." September took a small sip. She wasn't sure she should trust Angel, but it would be nice if they could at least be civil with each other. She pulled a slice of orange out of the glass and ate it. It had a slightly bitter after taste.

"It's fruit punch with a kick." Angel smiled, her dark red lipstick almost black in the dim light.

"It's got Everclear in it." Mattie took another sip. "You don't taste it, but it's really strong stuff."

"Watch out for the fruit." Kate whispered.

"Umm, thanks, Angel." If Kate and Mattie were drinking it, it couldn't be that bad. September took her glass and walked over to the couch. The couple had disappeared. September hoped they weren't in her bedroom. It had happened before. She sat down and Kate sat down beside her. "What's wrong with the fruit?"

"It soaks up the alcohol. You can get drunk just eating the fruit."

September drank half of her glass before setting it on the windowsill. Kate sat her glass down beside it. "If you can't taste the Everclear, what's that aftertaste it's got?"

"I don't know. It usually doesn't have that. Maybe some of the fruit isn't ripe. Maybe they made it with cheap fruit punch." Kate shrugged. "Do you want to dance?"

The makeshift dance floor was now almost full, so September and Kate stayed on the edge of the room and began dancing to an old Depeche Mode song. Halfway through the song, September began to feel warm and light-headed. She giggled and leaned in towards Kate. "I think the drink is kicking in."

Kate put a hand on her arm and nodded her head in agreement. They both giggled again. The skin where she touched September began to tingle. Everywhere Kate touched her felt electric, like her skin was plugged into a light socket. The room began to tilt, and September reached out to grab hold of Kate's arm. Kate pulled her closer and pressed herself up against September as they danced. September drew in a breath at how good it suddenly felt to have Kate touch her. Everywhere Kate's body brushed hers seemed to quiver and make September more aware of herself. Her breathing quickened and she felt the sudden urge to touch Kate. She wanted to touch Kate's hair, her arms, her mouth, her eyes, she wanted to touch her everywhere. Kate's skin was like living velvet.

She loved Kate for being her friend. She loved Mattie for throwing this party. She loved Gena for having a birthday. She even loved Angel for wanting a truce. She loved everyone and everything. She giggled at the thought.

She reached out and ran her hands down Kate's back, pulling her closer to her. Feeling an overwhelming desire, September leaned in and kissed Kate. Kate kissed her back, pushing her off the edge of the dance floor and up against the wall, narrowly missing the large sheet of paper with the marker hanging from it.

Angel and Mattie were in the kitchen opening more bags of potato chips and checking on the supply of ice, cups and jungle juice when Heather came into the kitchen. Heather leaned against the white Formica counter and grabbed a handful of chips.

"You said your roommate was straight." Heather accused Mattie as she got herself another cup of punch.

"She is." Angel had made the batch of jungle juice in the sink. Mattie reached in and grabbed a cherry and an orange slice.

Heather laughed. "Kate doesn't think so."

"What?"

"Go look." Heather grabbed another handful of chips and went back into the living room. Mattie looked at Angel, puzzled, and followed Heather into the living room. Angel got herself another glass of jungle juice before following her.

Mattie stopped in the center of the room and stared. Angel came up behind her and smiled. "Way to go, Kate."

September's back was to the wall, with Kate pressed up against her. They were kissing passionately. September's leg wrapped around Kate and her long, gauzy black skirt was hiked up to her thigh where Kate's hand disappeared underneath it. September pulled Kate closer with one hand while the other tangled in Kate's long blond hair. Kate's other hand had disappeared up the back of September's shirt.

Mattie and several of the other guests stood and watched them, until finally Mattie walked over and tapped September on the shoulder. She shrugged Mattie's hand off, and Mattie reached between them and grabbed September's chin. She forced September to look at her.

"You're causing a scene! What are you doing?"

September looked at Mattie and giggled. Her eyes were glassy. "Mattie, sweetheart, thanks for introducing me to Kate." She reached out and planted a kiss on Mattie's cheek. She looked at Kate. "Wanna go to my bedroom and see my tattoo?"

September played with a piece of Kate's hair and kissed her again. Kate nodded. They moved towards September's bedroom without letting go of each other. Mattie watched them leave the living room in silence.

Angel put an arm around Mattie and nibbled on her ear. When Mattie didn't respond, she stroked her hair. "What's wrong?"

"What a fucking hypocrite!" Mattie was furious.

"Who?" Angel slipped a hand under the edge of Mattie's tank top.

"September! She's high on something. They both are. How can she bitch at me about drugs and then get high and screw my old girlfriend! If she can do drugs, so can I." Responding to Angel's advances, Mattie turned towards Angel and kissed her lightly on the lips. "Got any X?"

"Of course, darling." Angel smiled and reached into her pocket.

Chapter 19

Kate squeezed her eyes closed more tightly, trying to block out the sun that was trying to invade her sleep. As she pulled the covers up trying to block the light, the sound of someone moving beside her brought her fully awake. She knew without looking that she wasn't in her own bed. Kate opened her eyes and the familiar movie posters and art prints that adorned September's walls greeted her. She winced at the bright sunlight streaming in through the curtains and shaded her eyes as she became aware of the pounding in her head. Kate groaned softly as she remembered the jungle juice she'd had at the party last night, even though she couldn't remember having more than one glass.

Lying still to try and ease her headache, Kate suddenly realized she was naked. Silently knowing and fearing what she would see, Kate turned her head and saw September, still sleeping, beside her. The arm tucked under September's chin told Kate she wasn't wearing anything either. Kate frantically thought back to the night before and suddenly remembered everything. September stirred next to her and woke up. She winced at the light and threw an arm over her eyes.

"God, how much did I drink last night?" September shifted to face Kate. "Um, Kate? How come I'm naked?"

"What do you remember about last night?" Kate lay quietly in the bed, waiting for September to answer.

September sat up, clutching the covers to her chest. She ran a hand through her hair and covered her face with her hand. She was silent for several moments. Kate, not knowing what to say, was silent also. Finally, September spoke. "What happened last night? I mean, I know what happened, but how-?"

September was whispering and the words sounded choked. Kate hesitantly reached out and touched September's back, relieved when she didn't pull away.

"I don't know." Kate broke off, unsure what to say. She'd never ended up in bed with a straight friend before.

September sighed. "Everything's kind of fuzzy. I remember we were dancing, and then we just started—."

"Making out on the dance floor. It's fuzzy for me too." Kate sat up and climbed out of the bed to her clothes. September turned her head away, embarrassed to see Kate naked, even if she had last night.

"How did we–I mean, we didn't drink that much. Did we?"

Kate handed September some clothes. "I only had one drink last night. You only had one drink. We've both had more than that without getting so drunk we ended up sleeping together. I don't know what happened. I guess that jungle juice must have been stronger than we thought."

"But everyone else was drinking the same thing." September couldn't believe one drink would do that to her.

"I know. I don't know what to say. I'm sorry, September. I feel like it's my fault."

"It's not your fault, Kate. I think it was my idea to come into my bedroom." September pulled the tank dress Kate handed her over her head, not paying any attention to the fact that she didn't have a t-shirt under it like usual, got out of bed, and began pacing the floor.

"I don't remember that part. It couldn't have been just the one drink." Kate shook her head and winced at the fresh burst of pain behind her temples.

"Yeah, I agree." September nodded her head and immediately regretted it as her head began pounding again. September sighed. "I've never acted like that in my life. I know you're right; it wasn't the one drink."

"It doesn't mean you're a lesbian. I'm not sure what happened, but—."

"Kate, it's okay. I don't blame you. I–why are you staring at me?" September sank down into the chair by her desk, frowning at Kate.

"Your shoulder." Kate knelt down beside September and gently touched the scar on her shoulder. "What happened to you?"

September was quiet for a moment. She couldn't tell Kate the entire truth right now. Her head wasn't working correctly, she wanted food and something to drink, and she wanted to kiss Kate again. She was so mixed up, she didn't want to talk about Lizzie. "I was in a car accident." She took a deep breath. "If it's okay with you, I've got a paper I need to get started on. I think I just want to eat something and try to get started."

"Oh, yeah, okay. I'll go." Kate turned at the door. "We're okay, right?"

"Of course." September smiled weakly.

Chapter 20

Spring turned on the porch light and looked through the peephole before opening the front door. "September? Sweetie, what are you doing here?" Spring gave her sister a hug and took a closer look at September's face. "Are you okay?"

"I don't know." September set her bag down and sat on the couch. She twisted the silver ring on her finger and hesitated before looking up at her sister. "Can I stay here for a couple of days? Without you telling mom or dad?"

"Of course. Do you want to talk about it?" If September didn't want their parents to know she was here, it must be serious. Spring sat down on the overstuffed couch beside her sister and rubbed September's back. September relaxed a little at the familiar ritual. When they were little, they shared a bedroom. Whenever September had nightmares or couldn't get to sleep, Spring would rub her back until she fell asleep.

"I'm not sure. I mean–I do, but I think I just want to go to bed right now." September had been trying to figure out how to talk to Spring about last night during the entire drive to Oklahoma. Her brain was in overdrive and the stress, and the drive home had worn her out.

Unable to concentrate on anything, needing to talk to someone, and feeling the urge to get out of town so she wouldn't run into Kate, September had finally thrown some clothes into a bag and jumped into her car at three o'clock that afternoon. She wasn't even sure where she was going until she was halfway to Spring's apartment. Spring had always been there for her, and she would help September figure out what was going on.

"Okay. You know where everything is. Mark's here, but if you change your mind about talking, I'll send him home."

"Thanks, Spring." September hugged her, picked up her bag and headed down the hall to the bathroom to change into her pajamas.

September took the folded pile of sweaters out of her drawer and put them in her suitcase. She couldn't wait to go home for Christmas break. Tony had driven down to Portales to help her pack. Before she could get more sweaters from her dresser, she felt hands massaging her shoulders.

"Why don't you take a break from packing?" Tony kissed her neck. September closed her eyes and relaxed against him.

"That feels good. I'll quit packing if you keep doing that." September smiled as the hands massaging her shoulders wrapped around her waist, pulling her close. Tony began gently biting her earlobe and neck.

She sighed as she enjoyed the sensations created by the hands exploring her body. This was different from Tony's usual idea of seduction. He rarely took the time to build her desire, so she was as excited about sex as he was. September's breath quickened as the hands roaming her body began unbuttoning her shirt. The feeling of skin on skin was erotic. By the time September's shirt was sliding down her shoulders to the floor, she was more aroused than she had ever been.

"You're never like this. What's gotten into you?" September opened her eyes and stared in surprise at the hands unbuttoning her jeans. She recognized the long, slender fingers with the short, frosted baby blue nails.

"K-Kate? What are–?" Kate silenced her with a kiss.

September gasped as she sat straight up in bed. She ran a hand through her hair and fell back against the pillows. Her blue flannel sheets were twisted into knots. God, the first sex dream she could ever remember having and Kate was in it.

She untwisted her sheets, rolled over, and tried to go back to sleep. It was impossible. She kept feeling Kate's hands on her body. She tossed and turned, fighting the fantasy building in her mind. Finally, she gave in, one hand sliding under her tank top to her hardening nipple and the other sliding into her flannel pajama pants and then lower, into her panties.

Spring had classes on Monday. September hung around the apartment for a while and then decided to go to the video store. Maybe she could rent some movies to help her answer some of the questions swirling around in her head. She could watch them while Spring was gone.

"Where'd you go?" Spring looked up from the book she was reading when September walked in the door. She saw the Blockbuster sack September set on the breakfast bar and marked her place in her book with her bookmark. "Are we having movie night? What did you get?"

"I felt like mindless comedy tonight. I got *Better Off Dead* and *Pump Up the Volume*." September tried to cover the bag with her coat.

"Both excellent choices, but it looks like you've got more than that in there." Spring picked up the bag and pulled the tapes out of the sack before September could stop her. There were three more movies in the sack. Spring looked at the titles and then at her younger sister. "*Better Than Chocolate* is really good, but I'm not sure *High Art* is one you need to see right now. I haven't seen this *2 Girls in Love*, but we can watch it together if you want to." Spring picked up all of the movies and carried them over to the TV. "We can watch any of them you want to."

September wasn't sure what to do. Spring was giving her the perfect opportunity to talk to her and didn't seem to be surprised or upset. She wasn't quite ready to talk though. She had intended to watch the other movies alone, while Spring was at work. Maybe watching one or two of them with Spring would help her open up to her sister. "Okay, I'll order a pizza and we'll watch the one neither of us has seen–if it's okay with you."

"You know I'm always up for pizza." Spring picked up the *2 Girls* movie and put it in the VCR.

September wiped the tears from her eyes and tried to catch her breath. She hadn't laughed that hard in a long time. Spring was trying to catch her breath too. September looked around the cozy living room she'd always felt so comfortable in. She had always been able to talk to Spring about anything. If she ever needed to talk to her sister, it was now. Spring's reaction to the movie told her she could talk to her about what had happened with Kate and Mattie and all the confusion she was going through. "Let's wait a little while for the next movie. I–I want to talk to you about something."

"Sure. What's going on?" Spring turned the television off and faced her little sister.

"I kissed Mattie at a party." September hadn't meant to jump right in, but the words tumbled out before she could stop them. "It was–we were playing truth or dare, and that girl, Angel, I told you about dared me to kiss her. Well, actually, she dared me to kiss the person in the room I was most attracted to."

"And that was Mattie?" Spring shifted positions on the couch.

"Well, sort of. I mean, everyone there was female, and I didn't want to kiss someone I didn't know, and Kate and I weren't getting along then, and she was really the only choice." September paused to take a breath. She glanced at Spring's face to see how she was taking her news so far. She had her sister's full attention, but there was no judgment or distaste on her face,

"And you liked it."

"Yeah, I did." September tucked her hair behind her ears. "I liked it a lot. I–I went to a lesbian club in Lubbock with her one night and this girl from the party was there. She tried to pick me up."

"Was she cute?"

September was stunned. She stared at Spring for a moment and then the two of them laughed. "She kind of was, but it freaked me out. I mean, I didn't know this girl and she was trying to rub up against me. And I was freaked out that she thought I was a lesbian just because I kissed Mattie at the party."

"You did say you were at a lesbian club."

"That's true." September paused for a moment. "I posed for Mattie a couple of months ago. It was–I was sitting there half-naked, and I really wanted her to kiss me again. I chickened out though. I thought she might read more into it than I wanted."

"What did you want?"

September hesitated before answering. This was the hard part. "I'm not sure. I've been reading her romance novels and I like them. Nobody had ever kissed me like she did. I wanted to feel that again. It was so different from Tony." September paused, not quite sure how to explain to Spring how Mattie's kiss had made her feel or how it was different.

"Was it better?" Spring reached for her drink on the coffee table. There was still something September wasn't telling her.

September was quiet. She had to be totally honest with Spring if she was going to get the advice she so desperately wanted. That meant being totally honest with herself, which was something she'd been trying to avoid. It was good to be with her sister, but running to Spring had changed her surroundings, not her situation. She took a deep breath. When she spoke again, Spring could barely hear her.

"Yes."

"It's okay to be attracted to a woman. If you liked kissing her, then you should explore that." Spring thought for a moment about the best way to bring up what she wanted to ask September. "Was Mattie the first woman you ever kissed?"

September seemed surprised by the question. "Of course. Why?"

"Well, it's just–you and Lizzie seemed so close. Dad and I kind of thought maybe you two were–."

"Me and Lizzie?" September was confused. "You and Dad thought Lizzie and I were together?"

"Well, yeah. You always had crushes on girls when you were little. We just thought you weren't ready to tell us yet. When Tony came into the picture, Dad thought he must have been wrong, and I thought maybe you were bisexual."

"But, why would you think–?" September couldn't finish her sentence. She was surprised and at the same time, the thought of her and Lizzie together didn't feel wrong.

"The way you looked at Lizzie. You looked at her the way Dad looks at Mom."

"Why didn't you say something to me?" September was shocked that her sister and father had realized she liked girls before she did. Why hadn't either of them said anything?

"I didn't know you didn't realize. I thought maybe you didn't want me to know. I thought maybe you being in love with Lizzie was why her death hit you so hard. I thought maybe you'd talk to me then, but when you didn't, I wasn't sure how to bring it up."

"In love with Lizzie? I–I don't–maybe." September clamped down on remembering the jealousy she'd felt when Lizzie had met her last boyfriend, and the tiny needle of truth she'd felt jab her when Kate had called Lizzie her girlfriend. She couldn't think about that right now if she was going to get everything out in the open with Spring. She still hadn't told her what had happened with Kate.

"Have you thought about trying to date a woman? Didn't you say Mattie belongs to some kind of group on campus?" Spring wasn't sure what to suggest next.

"I think there is, yes. There's something else." September paused and took a deep breath. "I–I slept with Kate at a party Friday night." Images of Kate caressing her crept into her head with that admission. September bit her lip and tried to push them out of her head.

"That's why you showed up the Saturday night." September's surprise visit suddenly made much more sense, but why her sister had sex with Kate when she was still struggling to accept her attraction to women didn't. September had always attached a lot of importance to sex and didn't sleep around casually. Spring paused for a moment. She didn't want to ask her next question, but she had to. "Did she–did you want to?"

September understood Spring's question. "She didn't force me. We–neither one of us is sure exactly what happened. I mean, she's cute, but I hadn't really–. We woke up in my bed Saturday morning and everything was hazy, but we remember what happened. We're just not sure how."

"Were you drunk?" Spring was concerned about this new revelation. Something didn't sound right about the situation.

"I don't think so." September looked unsure about her answer.

"What do you mean, you don't think so?"

"Friday night is kind of fuzzy, and I felt strange, but not like I was drunk. It was more like I was electrified." September pushed her hair off of her face as she struggled to explain the way she'd felt to Spring. "I felt light-headed and everywhere Kate touched me felt tingly. It was like she was touching me even when she wasn't touching me anymore. It was like there was this current running underneath my skin and I felt really good about everything and everybody."

"That sounds like you were rolling." Spring knew September wouldn't have taken the drug on her own. Somebody had to have given it to her without her knowledge.

"I didn't–I wouldn't–."

"I know. Think hard. Did you eat or drink anything at the party? Did Kate give you anything?"

"Kate wouldn't have drugged me. She was as confused as I was about what happened." September thought for a moment. "We only had one drink each. We had–." September sat up straighter and her hand flew over her mouth. "Oh my God! The drinks! Angel got our drinks for us. We were in the living room. She said it was a peace offering. She could've put anything she wanted to in them while she was in the kitchen!"

September couldn't believe what she had just figured out. It had to be what happened, but why would Angel do it? What was the point? Was the drug why she had enjoyed sleeping with Kate? Would she like sex with a woman if she wasn't on X? September wasn't sure she was ready to answer that honestly. She was still having problems accepting that she'd liked sleeping with Kate as much as she had. The new revelation that she'd been drugged was going to be a tough one to work through. She'd never been interested in drugs and having the choice taken away from her pissed her off. Especially after everything that had happened with Lizzie and Mattie.

"What are you going to do about it?"

"What can I do? The plastic cups have already been thrown away. It would just be her word against mine and Kate's and I'd have to tell people what happened. I'm not ready to tell people that I'm–that I slept with Kate. Portales is a small town. I don't want people staring at me and whispering when I walk across campus."

"Don't take anything else from her."

"I won't." The two sisters were silent for a few minutes. Then Spring smiled and playfully shoved September against the arm of the couch.

"So?"

"So what?" September tried unsuccessfully not to smile. She knew what Spring was asking.

"Kiss and tell. Was she any good?" Spring got up and ejected the film they had been watching out of the VCR. She picked up another movie and put it in the VCR.

"Well, all I have to compare it to is Tony, and I'm not sure how much the drug had to do with it, but–." September ducked her head so that her hair covered her face. "She made my toes curl. It was great."

Spring laughed. "Where did you get that expression? I'm glad you enjoyed it. Do you think it's something you'll want to do again?"

September thought about it for a moment before answering. "Yeah, I do. Not for a while though. I need to figure out how this fits in with who I am."

"What do you mean?"

"Well, I'm not ready to say I'm a lesbian, but the more books I read and movies I watch, the less Tony interests me. I'm not sure I'm bisexual, and I'm not sure I'm a lesbian, but if I'm being honest, I'm pretty sure I'm not straight."

"Well, that's a step in the right direction." Spring put an arm around her sister and hugged her. "I'm glad you came to see me. I hope I helped."

"You did. I just needed someone to listen to me as I said it all out loud. Do you think Mom and Dad will be okay with this when I'm ready to tell them?"

"Yeah, I do. They just want you to be happy. Besides, they did grow up with the whole free love era." Spring paused. "Does this mean you're leaving soon?"

"I should get back. I'm missing classes and I left without telling anyone I was going. Kate will be worried about me. She's probably tried to call a million times."

"Okay, this is the last movie then." Spring pressed play on the remote.

September and Spring had just started the second movie when the doorbell rang. They looked at each other. Spring wasn't expecting anyone, and no one knew September was there.

"I'll be right back." Spring headed for the front door as September paused the movie. She wondered who could be at the door. It was late for visitors, and Mark had left that morning for a job interview in Dallas. She quickly turned off the VCR and hid the movie boxes when she heard the familiar voices in the entryway.

"Mom? Dad, what are you doing here? What's wrong?" Spring stepped back to let her parents inside. Her mother's eyes were red, like she'd been crying. Her father had deep stress lines marring his forehead, and his normally carefree blue eyes were full of worry.

"September's missing." Their mother sounded like she was about to start crying again.

"What do you mean, she's missing?"

"Kate called us looking for her. She's been trying to get a hold of September for two days. She went to the house and Mattie told her the bed hasn't been slept in and she hasn't seen her."

"Well, maybe she–."

"Her car's gone, and Kate said September wasn't in any of her classes today." Their father was holding onto his composure, but Spring could tell he was just as worried as her mother was.

"I'm sure she's fine."

Their mother grabbed Spring's shoulders. "Have you heard from her? Has she–?"

September sighed as she stood up. She couldn't do this to her parents. She hadn't meant to cause all this panic. Ever since Lizzie's death, her parents worried whenever she wasn't right on time. She hadn't thought Kate would try to call her home. She stepped into the entryway. "Mom, I'm fine."

September's mother grabbed her and hugged her tightly. "Thank God! I thought–how could you disappear like that without telling anyone? Especially after everything that happened last year!"

September's father ran a hand over his daughter's hair and kissed her forehead. She knew without a word from him how worried he'd been. She took his hand and held onto it.

"I'm sorry. I didn't mean to scare anyone." September wasn't sure she could take this. They were overreacting and she wasn't sure she could calm them down without telling them what was wrong. She didn't want to tell them.

"Why didn't you tell us your sister was here?" Their mother turned on Spring.

"Mom, don't yell at her. I asked her not to." September sighed. "Let's go sit down."

September's father kept his hold on her hand as the whole family sat down in Spring's living room. September glanced down. The sight of her father's right index finger with the first joint missing reminded her again of how important she and Spring were to him. She remembered when he'd had the accident. She was ten. She and Spring had run into his workshop after school to show him their papers. They'd startled him and the saw blade slipped. He'd been more concerned with making sure Spring and September didn't blame themselves for the slip than he was about his finger.

"Did something happen? Why are you skipping classes?" September's mother wasn't giving up. September let her mother rant. She didn't want to tell them why she was in Oklahoma, but she didn't want to lie to them either.

"Nothing happened. I just needed to get away for a few days. I'm going back tomorrow." That much was true. She had decided to go back to school the next day.

"Are you sure? Kate said something happened." September's mother was about to drive her crazy. She usually respected her daughters' privacy without having to be asked, but her concern about September had her acting in ways she normally wouldn't.

"Mom, I am fine. If I didn't hurt myself last year, I'm not going to hurt myself now." September paused and took a deep breath. Her mother would never admit it, but September knew that was what she was most concerned about. "Something did happen, but I don't want to talk about it with you. I wanted to talk to Spring, and I wanted to get away from the situation for a few days. I know I shouldn't have skipped classes and I won't do it again." She kissed her mother's cheek when she started to open her mouth. "I promise."

"September, if it's bad enough that you–."

"Brenda, she said she didn't want to talk about it. She's fine. Let's go home and let the girls get some sleep." September's father squeezed her hand and kissed both of his daughters before standing up. "Call us when you get home tomorrow, okay, pumpkin?"

Chapter 21

Kate rubbed the last bit of sleep from her eyes as she hurried through the living room to open the door. She had no idea who would be knocking on her door at eight in the morning on a Saturday. She stared in surprise for a moment before finding her voice. "Hi, stranger."

Even though September had said she didn't blame Kate for what had happened the night of Gena's birthday party, the two of them had avoided each other for the past week. September had called her with her suspicions about Angel spiking their drinks, but they hadn't seen each other. It was as much Kate's choice as September's. Kate was having far too many dreams about what it had been like to caress her soft skin and run her fingers through September's silky hair. She could still feel September's lips on hers. The warmth she felt flood her chest at the sight of September standing in her doorway in jeans and a white t-shirt told Kate she was asking for trouble.

"Hi." September eyed Kate's blue terry cloth robe. "I woke you up, didn't I? I'll come back later." She turned to go. Kate reached out and placed her hand on her arm to stop her. September felt her heart beat faster at Kate's touch.

"No, it's okay. Come on in." Kate moved out of the doorway to let September through.

September was always amazed at how unlike a rented apartment Kate's place looked. The walls were painted a soft blue color and there were framed Georgia O'Keefe prints and photos of dancers on the walls. A rug that wicked up the colors in the prints lay on the hardwood floor. A matching blanket rested across the back of the off-white couch. Oversized throw pillows and an overstuffed chair carried on the soft teal and rose colors. All of Kate's coffee and end tables matched. A small, framed picture of Mattie's hung over the back of the couch.

September sat down on the couch. She was nervous. She caught herself staring at Kate's mouth and quickly looked away. "I—can I ask you something?"

"Sure." Kate sat down on the couch beside her, careful not to let her leg touch September's. "Is something wrong?"

"Yes, no—I don't know. Ever since the party, I've been thinking." Kate sat quietly, waiting for September to continue, not daring to hope that September wanted to kiss her again.

"How did you know?" September couldn't look at Kate. She let her long hair fall to hide her face like a curtain.

"Know what?" Kate's heart beat faster as she pushed a stray piece of blond hair out of her face.

September took a deep breath. She'd decided she needed to talk to a lesbian about this. She had questions only a woman who loved women could answer. She had thought about talking to Mattie, but she looked so much like Lizzie, and she was so out of it lately, she didn't think she would be able to ask all of her questions or get the answers she wanted. She didn't know who else to talk to, but the idea of looking into Kate's blue eyes while she asked intimate questions made her nervous. "How did you know you liked girls?"

Kate smiled. Sure that September was going to hear her heart beating, she took a deep breath. "I was in high school. My best friend was a couple of years older than I was. She told me she was a lesbian and she'd talk to me about girls she had crushes on. When she went to college, she wrote me a letter about this girl she'd met. I suddenly realized I was jealous, and that was ridiculous because she was my best friend. I wanted her to be happy. I drove out to visit her one weekend, we went to a party, and I kissed her. That was all it took. When I look back now, I can see that I always had crushes on girls, but it wasn't obvious to me till then."

"So, you always knew?" September whispered.

"Deep down, I guess I did, but I had boyfriends in high school."

"Did you ever sleep with any of them?"

"No. I never wanted to, and they never tended to last long. I always found something wrong with them before we got that far." Kate paused, trying to decide the best way to talk to September about her sexuality without upsetting her. "You know, just because we–." Kate searched for a tactful way to say what she wanted to say. "Just because I saw your tattoo doesn't mean you're a lesbian, especially considering we were both flying at the time."

September looked at her hands. She couldn't look at Kate and say what she wanted and needed to say. "I never really liked sex. I wasn't interested in sex in high school. I finally slept with Tony to get it over with because I was tired of being a virgin, but I never really enjoyed it." She took a deep breath. "I've been reading Mattie's romance novels and I–I liked sleeping with you. I liked it a lot. I liked it when Mattie kissed me, and I wanted her to do it again. I even tried to get her to do it again by posing for her. I just–I couldn't admit it to myself." She paused and then added, "I really wasn't trying to break you and Mattie up, but I can see now why you might have felt that way. I'm sorry."

Kate thought her heart was going to beat out of her chest if it sped up anymore. September liked sex with her. There was actually a chance this wasn't just an ill-advised crush on a straight girl. Kate tried to push those thoughts aside to give September what she needed, and not what Kate wanted.

"Thank you for that. Mattie and I breaking up was the right thing though. It's okay to be questioning your sexuality. I'm glad you're talking to me about it. Reading those books is a good place to start. When or if you ever think you want to, there's a group on campus. I could take you to one of their meetings. It's kind of like a support group and they do activities and things." Kate reached out and touched September's arm against her better judgment. "I can take you to a gay club if you want. Just let me know."

"I don't think I want to go to one of those meetings and I know I don't want to go to a gay club again, at least not yet. I just wish–." September ran hand through her hair and sighed. "I just wish Mattie hadn't started dating Angel so soon. Maybe if she hadn't, I could've talked to her and told her–." September stopped when she realized what she was about to admit. Kate studied September's face for a moment and tried to ignore the stabbing pain in her chest as the truth hit her.

"You like her, don't you?"

September didn't say anything. She didn't know the answer.

Chapter 22

Kate and September managed to get over their awkwardness with each other and September had invited Kate over to hang out before they both got too busy with midterms and packing for Christmas break. They had been avoiding Mattie, and it seemed like she had been avoiding them too. They were surprised when she knocked on September's door and burst in.

"There you are! Oh good, Kate's here too!" Mattie had her camera around her neck, her camera bag on her shoulder and an armful of props and costumes. "I could really use your help. Millie managed to get me permission to use the sets for Chicago for a photo shoot I want to do but the director said it has to be tonight and half of my models are out of town. Can you help me? Please!"

"What's the idea? You know my naked rule." Kate put down her magazine and looked at Mattie.

"What's your naked rule?" September laughed.

"If a bikini covers it, she can't show it in a picture." Kate took a drink of her soda.

"That's a good rule. I want that rule too." September popped her last cracker in her mouth.

"Greg decided to make us draw subjects and time periods for our midterm assignment. I got couples and the nineteen twenties. The Chicago set gets torn down tomorrow so the director said Millie could let me in to use it and she can let me use the costumes." Mattie paused. "I thought since you two were friends now and you—well, I thought maybe you would be one of my couples."

September and Kate looked at each other. Mattie seemed really excited about the photo shoot and sounded like she'd really thought about it. It had been a while since she had been that interested in an assignment. It seemed like a sign Mattie was turning things around. September shrugged. She was willing if Kate was,

"What do you say? Wanna let me grab your ass for the sake of art?" Kate joked.

"Sure. Why not?" September looked at Mattie. "What do you need us to do?"

"If you can do your makeup with a smoky eye and dark red lips, hair parted on the side, and if you have a pair of plain black heels, bring them. Kate, bring your Mary Jane heels if you still have them, and meet me at the theater at seven." Mattie headed out the door, paused, and turned back. "Thank you. I really appreciate you helping out."

September and Kate had to hurry if they wanted to get ready on time. Kate ran to her apartment to grab her make-up and the heels Mattie had asked her to bring. September put some curls in her hair while she waited for Kate. They did their make up together and decided to drive to the theater since they weren't sure how long they would be there.

"Oh, just in time." Mattie greeted them at the theater door. "Angel and Gena are already here, so I'm going to get started with them while you get dressed." September followed Kate and Mattie back to the costume room. "Millie, Give both of them garters and necklaces. I want Kate in the blue bra and tap pants set she wore in the show, and September in the chemise with the lace shoulder inserts."

She put a hand on September's shoulder and leaned in so only September could hear her. "The lace should cover your scar. I can also try to shoot so that shoulder doesn't show if it's not covered completely."

"Thanks." September smiled at her, took what seemed like a small bit of fabric from Millie, and went to find a place to change in the dressing room.

September stared at herself in the mirror. The pale pink chemise with cream lace insets was pretty, and Mattie was right. Her scar was completely covered by the lace. She breathed a sigh of relief. Mattie and Kate had both seen it, but none of the other people here had, and she definitely didn't want to explain it to Angel. Mattie seemed more like the girl she'd met at the fountain than she had in a while. She wanted this photo shoot to go well for Mattie. Fighting with Angel wouldn't help her accomplish that. She was just glad she didn't have to pose with Angel.

"Wow." September jumped at the sound of Kate's voice. She had been so caught up in thinking, she hadn't noticed Kate walking up behind her. "You look amazing."

"Thanks. You do too." September swallowed. The sky-blue color made Kate's eyes even bluer, and the black lace popped against her creamy, pale skin. The bralette showed just enough of Kate's cleavage and plenty of her toned stomach.

"Mattie said she's ready for us."

They walked onto the stage area together. September had to admit Angel looked amazing with her hair slicked back in a twenties inspired suit with the tie hanging loose around her neck and the shirt mostly unbuttoned. They stood quietly at the edge of the stage while Mattie pulled a fainting couch to the middle of the bedroom set. Mattie motioned to them.

"September, I want you to sit here sideways. Lean back with your front foot on the floor and the back foot on the couch. Kate, kneel on the couch in front of her with your back hand on the arm of the couch, and grab her necklace with your other hand. Pull it up like you're using it to pull her towards you for a kiss. September, put your front hand on her shoulder and grip her bra strap like you're also pulling her towards you." Mattie circled around them clicking pictures as she gave instructions on how she wanted them to move.

"Okay, that's enough of those. Millie, can you move the bedroom wall and pull in the jail set?" Mattie waved the two of them towards the side of the stage. "Take five while we get this set up."

September went back into the green room to get a drink of water. When she walked back into the backstage area, she got partway on stage and froze. A section of jail bars was center stage. Kate was holding onto the bars and swinging her hips in time to the music September finally noticed. *God, she looks sexy. I am in so much trouble here.* Mattie saw her and waved her over. September walked slowly, trying to let her heartbeat slow and get a handle on the hormones she barely recognized, let alone know how to control.

"Okay, I need both of you over here. Kate, put your back to the bars. September, I want you to reach this hand over her shoulder and brace yourself on the bar. Don't worry, they're stable. Kate, put your opposite foot up on the bar. September, get closer and wrap your front leg around Kate, higher if you can get it. Kate, wrap your arm around her waist and grab her ass with your front hand." Mattie was giving them directions, occasionally helping move them into position.

Kate's face was inches away from September. Her eyes dropped to September's lips before moving back up to her eyes. "Are you okay with that?"

"It's for art, right?" September managed to get the words out and avoid staring at Kate's mouth. She couldn't contain the small gasp she made when Kate followed through on Mattie's instruction.

Kate's blue eyes darkened with the sound, and a small smirk appeared. She gripped September's ass harder and pulled her hips closer. September's lips parted as she just barely managed to suppress a small moan. The snapping of the camera became more frantic as Mattie tried to keep up with what she was getting from the two of them.

"Can I kiss you?" Kate whispered in September's ear as Mattie circled them.

September swallowed. "Please." She met Kate halfway and they kissed.

Her elbow bent, causing September to crash into Kate, pushing her up against the bars. Her leg lowered to keep her upright as Kate rolled them so September was the one with her back to the bars.

"Holy shit. That's hot. I guess I did you two a favor." Angel's voice pulled them back to the stage set and September realized she couldn't hear Mattie's camera anymore. Mattie was staring at them with a look on her face September couldn't quite read.

"Thanks. That was-that was great. I definitely got some good shots." Mattie stood there, staring at them for a moment before she turned and hurried towards her camera bag.

September slipped out from between Kate and the bars and headed to the dressing room to change her clothes. Mattie met her at the dressing room door, when she came out.

"Hey, I just wanted to say thank you again for helping me. You-you and Kate looked great. Those pictures are going to be gorgeous." Mattie paused, took a deep breath, and put her hand on September's arm. "I really appreciate you helping me, especially after that argument we had. I really am sorry about that."

"I know, but thanks for the apology. I appreciate it." September was glad to hear Mattie apologizing, but she was distracted. She hadn't expected or intended to make out with Kate, especially not in front of Mattie. She gave Mattie a hug and headed towards the car.

Chapter 23

Christmas break had come just in time. All of the soul-searching September had been doing had made her realize that while she hadn't meant to, she had cheated on Tony, and he didn't deserve that. She needed to talk to him. She also needed a break from seeing Mattie and Kate to see if she could untangle all the feelings she had jumbled up inside. She was really looking forward to being home. Her excitement mounted the closer she got to her neighborhood.

"September! Honey, you're home!" Her mother came rushing out to meet Spring's car and hugged her tightly as she got out of the car.

"Hi, Mom. It's good to see you." September hugged her mother back. "Hi, Dad." She disentangled herself from her mother as her father came outside. She hugged her dad, and he gave her a tight squeeze, holding her tightly for several moments. She had always been daddy's girl and he missed her.

"Let's get your bags and bring them inside. We've got you for almost three weeks. We can talk in the house." September glanced at Spring, and then put one arm around her mother and the other around her dad as she gently steered them towards the house.

"I kind of thought I'd stay at Spring's apartment with her. She wants me to help her with the wedding plans and I'll be over there a lot. It would just be easier to stay there." Staying with Spring also ensured more privacy if she wanted to talk to her about Kate or Mattie.

"If that's what you girls want. We'll miss having you here though." September's dad kissed her cheek. They all went inside and sat on the couch. September's mother had a plate of Christmas cookies on the coffee table. September reached for one and bit the head off a Santa Claus.

"I thought you were going to wait for me to bake the cookies." Baking Christmas cookies together was part of the Ellis family tradition.

"It was my turn to bring refreshments to the gallery staff meeting. We'll bake some more tomorrow if you want." September's dad brought in mugs of hot chocolate and set it on the table. September reached over, took one, and handed it to Spring before taking one for herself.

"Of course, I want to. It's tradition." September looked around the living room she'd spent so much of her childhood in. It still seemed as warm and homey as always with her mom's artwork on the walls and her sculptures on the tables and the fireplace mantle her father had carved himself, but the feeling the world couldn't touch her had disappeared. She was becoming more and more aware of the fact that she was very lucky to have the family she had. September had never felt like she had grown up. Sitting on her parents' couch with cookies and cocoa made her feel like a child, but she realized that dealing with Lizzie's death and Mattie's drug use had killed the feeling of being a child pretending she was an adult.

Her parents had waited for her to come home before decorating the tree. She hadn't really been feeling the Christmas spirit, but maybe decorating the tree together would help. September got up, found her favorite holiday music CD and put it in the stereo. Her father got up to help her untangle the lights like they did every year. While they did that, Spring and her mother began unpacking the decorations.

"Are you sure you want to do this tonight?" Her dad handed her a bulb to replace one that had burned out in the strand she was working on.

"I've been sitting in the car for hours. Standing will be nice for a while."

She helped her father put the twinkling blue lights on the live pine tree her parents had selected. Once the lights were on, the next part of the family ritual began. Each one of them had a box that held special ornaments. Those were the ones that went on first. September ran her fingers over the ornaments in her box. There were ornaments people had given her parents when she was a baby, elementary school projects, and ornaments she had made when she was learning how to do beadwork. Her fingers trembled as she came across the one ornament she'd been both looking for and dreading.

She gently lifted the delicate spun glass angel out of its cotton and held it up to the light. She wasn't sure she wanted to put it on the tree this year. The angel had been a present from Lizzie. She stood and stared at the angel in her hand. She didn't want to see it every time she looked at the tree, but she wasn't sure she could bring herself not to hang it on the tree. Her father took the angel from her and gently laid it back in its cotton. He put an arm around her and gave her a squeeze.

"Why don't you leave it in the box for now if you're not sure? I'm sure Lizzie would understand. You can always get it out later and hang it on the tree if you decide you want to."

September smiled even as her eyes welled with tears. She nodded and kissed his cheek. He was right.

Chapter 24

September had been home for a week, and she had been dodging Tony the entire time, trying to work up the nerve to talk to him. She was at her parents' house, getting ready for Christmas dinner. Her mom was busy at the gallery with last minute Christmas Eve sales, so she had volunteered to cook. Cooking was helping distract her from the gnawing feeling that she should have broken up with Tony sooner. She knew she hadn't because she felt guilty about breaking up with him after he had stood by her and her family last year and given her so much support while she was in the hospital and undergoing physical therapy.

"Look who's here." September's dad walked into the kitchen where September was cooking dinner with Tony following behind him.

"Hi, baby, it's good to see you." Tony grabbed her and swung her around. He kissed her and ran his hands over her hair. "I missed you."

The sight of him was like a punch in the stomach. September wasn't sure what she wanted in the way of her love life, but she did know she couldn't go on letting Tony think things were good between them. She was pretty sure he loved her, but she was also positive she didn't love him. Talking to him on the phone and opening his letters had started to feel like a chore and if she loved him, it should be something she enjoyed.

God, she really didn't want to hurt him. He had been there for her when she needed him. He had slept at the hospital more times than she could count. He didn't deserve to be dumped, but he didn't deserve to be strung along either. September set the timer for the lasagna and wiped her hands off on a towel.

"Hi, Tony. I'm glad you're here. We need to talk." September took a deep breath and took his arm. She grabbed her coat, led him outside to the backyard and sat down on the porch swing. Tony sat down beside her and took her hands in his.

"Listen, baby, Kelly and Alan want us to go ice skating with them tomorrow and my roommate's out of town, so I thought–."

"Tony, please. I need to talk to you. It's important. Will you just listen to me?" September looked at him and almost lost her nerve. He was looking at her with such tenderness. She was going to crush him, and right before Christmas. She had to do it now. She was going to go visit Kate for New Year's Eve and she didn't want Tony hanging over her head when she went.

"Sure, baby. What is it?" Tony gave her his full attention.

"I've been thinking, and I think it might be a good idea if we see other people." The words came out in a rush. September took a breath. "I'm going to school in another state, we never see each other anymore. I think it might be better for both of us."

"Why would you say that? I hate not seeing you every day, but I love you. I don't want to date anyone else." Tony put his hand on her cheek. September took his hand away and put it in his lap. She couldn't look at him and say the next thing she had to say.

"But I think I do. No, I know I do. Lately, I've been attracted to other people. I want to go out with them if they ask me." September paused, and bit her lip. "You're a great guy, Tony, and you deserve a girl who feels the same way about you that you do about her. I'm just not that girl. I don't feel the same way about you that I used to."

"But, baby, I love you. I know you love me too!"

"No, I don't. I'm sorry, Tony. I don't want to hurt you, but I can't keep letting you think our relationship is something it's not."

The tears in his eyes stunned September. She hadn't thought he would cry. She felt tears stinging her own eyes. She pulled her hands away from Tony and turned her head away from him. They sat there in silence for a few moments. She felt Tony get up and heard him go back inside the house.

September stayed in the porch swing, staring out across the backyard without really seeing it. She felt someone sit down beside her and put an arm around her. She knew it was her dad. She leaned against him as a tear ran down her cheek.

"Hey, Pumpkin. Talk to your old man. What's going on in that head of yours?" He gave her a gentle squeeze and kissed the top of her head.

"I broke up with Tony." September longed to be able to crawl into her father's lap and tell him everything like she had when she was little. Back then, he could always make everything okay. She couldn't tell him about all her confusion over Mattie and Kate and her questions about her sexuality. She didn't understand it herself; she didn't know how she would make him understand.

"What happened?" Her father's voice was gentle. He would accept whatever she told him as the truth.

"I just don't feel the same way about him anymore. I'm so confused, Dad. There's just so much going on. I thought going away would make everything simpler. It just made a bigger mess of things, and now I've hurt Tony. I didn't want to do that." September buried her face in her father's coat, inhaling the familiar smell of wood and Aramis cologne that was ingrained in her memories of him.

"He did look pretty upset when he left."

"I didn't think he'd take it that hard. I guess I figured he might have been feeling the distance too."

"Well, I think you did the right thing. If you don't love him, he should know. He'll be glad you told him in time."

"Thanks, Dad. I wish I didn't feel so rotten about it."

"I know, Pumpkin, I know." Her father sat there silently with September leaning against his shoulder for a few moments. "You know, September, your mom and I love you, and as long as they treat you with respect, anyone you want to bring home will be welcome in this house. Anyone at all."

September hugged her father tightly and kissed him on his cheek. She knew what he was trying to tell her, and she appreciated it. She knew Spring hadn't told her parents anything September had talked to her about. She didn't know what to say about what her father had said, so she just kissed him again and went inside to check on the lasagna.

Chapter 25

Spring walked into the bedroom September had been staying in with a flat, brightly wrapped package in her hands. She sat down on the bed next to September's suitcase.

"I've got one more present for you. It's not exactly a Christmas present and I didn't think you'd want to open it in front of mom and dad." Spring handed September the package. September stopped packing her bag for her trip to Kate's and took the present from her sister.

"Another present? But you already gave me the painting, that dress, and those two CDs." September looked at Spring quizzically. Her sister was smiling at her in a strange way. Spring was up to something.

"Just open it. It's something I came across while I was shopping, and I thought you should have it."

September sat down on the bed beside Spring and unwrapped the present. She stared at it for a moment and then looked back up at her sister. "You just happened to come across a book called *The Joy of Lesbian Sex*? Why are you giving this to me? I still don't even know whether I want Mattie or Kate."

"I thought Mattie was dating Angel. I thought you were interested in Kate."

"Well, I am interested in Kate, but Lizzie's doing really well–."

"Did you hear what you just said? Sweetie, Lizzie's dead. Mattie is the one you're thinking about. Right?" Spring moved closer and put an arm around September.

"I said Mattie. I–didn't I? God, I don't know. I'm so confused." Mattie's physical resemblance to Lizzie still threw her sometimes. She caught herself thinking Mattie liked the same things Lizzie had.

"Maybe you just think you're attracted to Mattie because she looks so much like Lizzie." Spring smoothed her younger sister's hair from her face.

"I don't know. I don't think so. I mean, her kiss is what started all this for me. I can't believe you bought me this book." September stared down at the book in her hands. She opened it, flipped through a few pages, and quickly closed it when she realized how explicit it was. She couldn't believe what her sister had given her. It scared and excited her at the same time. It was definitely something she never would have bought for herself.

"The book is for when you are ready. I just want you to be safe. And I did just find it. I was looking for a copy of the Kama Sutra for my honeymoon." Spring winked at September. "Just read it, okay? Who knows, maybe it will make you horny enough to jump Kate while you're there." Spring laughed and hugged her sister to let her know she was teasing. September giggled in spite of herself and gently tapped Spring with her book.

"You have sex on the brain! Ever since you met Mark, you have been such a sex fiend."

"Sex is fun. You should enjoy it. Promise me you'll read the book, and when the time comes, you'll use it."

September sighed. She wasn't getting out of this until she promised. She hoped someday that she would feel the same way about sex that Spring did. She hadn't told her sister this, but the only time she'd had an orgasm with another person was with Kate. She wouldn't admit it to Spring, but the book did interest her. She would have to take a good look at it when she knew she wouldn't be disturbed.

She wasn't sure when that would be. She was going to a party at the gallery with her family tonight, and tomorrow she was driving to Albuquerque to see Kate for New Year's Eve. She was going to have to hide the book in her suitcase. She definitely didn't want Kate to see it.

Chapter 26

"Want another drink?"

"Sure." September nodded. "I'll stay here to keep our spot." September waved Kate towards the crowded bar. She'd gone to the lesbian bars with Spring a couple of times over Christmas break and had gotten over staring. The crowd at the bar on New Year's was especially rowdy and September was having fun. She and Kate had arrived early and were planning on seeing the sunrise on the new year.

Kate watched September dance while she waited in line at the bar. She had gone all out tonight and looked beautiful. Kate had already had to fend off more than one would-be suitor by telling them she was September's girlfriend.

September was wearing body-hugging black pleather pants Kate had seen hanging in her closet but had never seen her wear. She had shocked Kate by wearing a silver lame top held on only by strings that crossed her back twice before tying in a knot midway down her back. The scar Kate knew had more of a story and that September usually kept hidden was on full display, but September didn't seem to care. The knowledge that there was no way September was wearing a bra made Kate weak in the knees. September had pinned her hair up to expose her bare back and had applied more eye makeup than Kate had ever seen her wear. She looked wild and sexy, and Kate had almost made up her mind to kiss her at midnight.

Kate brought their drinks back to September on the dance floor. She was flirting with a girl in a black minidress, but when Kate reappeared, September put an arm around her, hugged her, and the girl disappeared.

"I feel so not like me tonight. I think I might actually like clubbing!" September laughed and took a drink from her glass. She caught sight of the large screen showing the countdown in Times Square and pointed. "Look! It's almost midnight!"

The music changed and Prince's 1999 began pumping through the speakers. Kate pressed up against September and danced closer to her as the dance floor got even more crowded. People began counting down and Kate and September stopped dancing and stood with their arms wrapped around each other as the crush of people got even stronger and dancing became almost impossible.

Horns blared, confetti and balloons fell from the ceiling and before Kate could say anything, September kissed her hard on the mouth. Kate felt September's tongue slide against hers. She pulled her closer and kissed her back. They kissed until the end of the song. Finally, Kate broke the embrace. "I'm glad you came to see me."

"Me too." September smiled at her.

They danced until the club turned the lights on and told the remaining partiers that they didn't have to go home, but they couldn't stay there. Laughing, the two made their way to September's car.

September reached into her pocket for the car keys. Since she had stopped drinking right after midnight, she was going to drive them back to Kate's house. The keys were gone. She checked her pockets again, but still didn't turn up any keys. "Hurry and open the door, it's cold!" Kate was hugging herself and bouncing up and down to keep warm.

"Kate, do you have the keys? I don't have them."

"What? I don't have any pockets." Kate walked around the Camaro to the driver's side door and joined September in trying to see inside the car. The keys were lying on the floor of the driver's seat. "Damn! How are we going to get in? It's two o'clock in the morning."

"How much money do you have left? Maybe we can call a cab." September pulled two crumpled ones out of her pocket. She checked the pocket she'd been holding Kate's money in and came up with three more dollars and some change.

"My dad and Lindsey will kill us if I call and wake them up."

"You may not have a choice. We don't have any money."

"Can I help you ladies?" The bouncer had been watching them stand beside the car and decided to see if there was a problem.

"We locked our keys in the car."

"I can help." The three turned to see who had spoken. A drag queen in a red dress they had seen earlier was standing beside the car. "These cars are really easy to break into."

September and Kate looked at each other. "I don't want to know how you know that, but if you can help us get the keys, we'd appreciate it."

"Luckily, you have an older car. See how there's a flat space between the edge of the window seal and the window? Okay, when I tell you to, I want you to slide your arm in the window and unlock the door. These windows will actually stretch about eight inches without breaking." The drag queen was looking at September. She nodded and watched in amazement as she slipped her fingers into the crack she had just pointed out between the car's frame and the window and slowly began working her way towards the top of the window, pulling it out as she did so. "Now."

September slipped her arm inside the window and down to the lock. She unlocked the door, and the drag queen opened the door, freeing her arm. "Thank you so much! You're a lifesaver!"

"No problem. I'm always happy to help out family, especially when the couple are as adorable together as you two are." Kate and September glanced at each other. They both opened their mouths to correct her, but the queen was already climbing into a waiting car. They waved and watched their helper pull out of the parking lot.

"What a way to start the new year." September and Kate got into the car and turned the heat up. "It's going to make a great story though." The two of them laughed, and Kate directed September to her house. They quietly let themselves in and got ready for bed.

Kate came out of the bathroom in her pajamas. She climbed into bed beside September and leaned over to tell her good night. "I had a great time. You looked amazing. What made you decide to wear that?" September didn't answer. Kate looked over and realized she was already asleep. She leaned over and gently kissed her cheek. "Night."

Chapter 27

Despite their kiss on New Year's, nothing had happened when September and Kate went back to Eastern. Kate had asked September to go out to dinner to celebrate her birthday. She had been planning on asking September on a proper date, but Mattie had contacted her and asked for her help in throwing September a surprise party so instead Kate's date plans turned into getting her out of the house so Mattie could decorate, and people could arrive.

"Thanks for dinner and the movie, Kate." Kate had taken September to Cattle Baron, one of the few nicer restaurants in Portales, for her twenty-second birthday. Since most of their meals involved steak, September ended up with pasta and a salad. Kate had some fish that she said was good, but September thought it looked overcooked. They left the restaurant without dessert or having anyone sing happy birthday. September was relieved to have escaped that particular form of birthday torture. The romantic comedy they went to see was funny, but the ending was predictable.

September pulled her coat tighter around the black scoop-neck top and long, fitted gray skirt she was wearing. She felt a chill with every step she took on the side of the skirt with the knee-high slit and was glad they were almost to her house. She couldn't hear any music, but someone must have been having a party, because she and Kate had to park down the block from her house.

The moonlit walk with Kate was almost romantic and could have been a date if either one of them had just admitted it. September could tell Kate liked her and had almost made up her mind to try and kiss Kate once they reached her house. She knew she was attracted to both Mattie and Kate, but Mattie wasn't free, and she kept dreaming about the night she and Kate slept together. Kate was cute, and she was a great kisser. September wondered what the sex would be like if they weren't on drugs, although she wasn't sure she was ready to go there again. As they walked up the sidewalk to her house, September noticed the lights were out. "It looks like Mattie may have actually vacated for a while. Do you want to come in?"

"Sure." Kate held the screen door open for September while she fumbled with her keys out of nervousness and finally unlocked the door. She reached inside and switched on the light before stepping inside.

"Surprise!" The living room was full of September's friends. Kate gave her a gentle push and stepped inside behind her. September turned and hugged Kate.

"Was this your idea?"

"No. It was all Mattie's." September looked around the room for Mattie but didn't see her. Balloons and streamers decorated the house. As she walked through the decorated living room, friends hugged her and wished her a happy birthday. September saw a table in the corner with colorfully wrapped packages and a purple and white frosted birthday cake. She walked towards the cake to read the inscription when Mattie and Angel came out of the hallway and into the living room.

"Happy birthday! I was hoping I'd get your present wrapped before you got here." Mattie hugged September. She hugged Mattie back tightly. In honor of the occasion, Mattie was wearing a dress in place of her usual jeans.

"You didn't have to get me a present and throw me a party."

"Come on, let's get you a drink." Mattie linked her arm through September's and led her through the party guests to the kitchen.

"Kate, do you want one too?"

"Not right now. I'm going to go ask Mandy something about class. I'll be back in a minute." Kate was trying to give September time with Mattie even though she didn't want to.

"Okay." She followed Mattie into the kitchen. September dropped ice into two glasses and set them on the counter. Mattie poured a generous amount of rum and Coke into each one.

"I'm glad you moved in." Mattie held up her glass.

"Me too." September clinked her glass against Mattie's and took a drink. Things had been going well since she and Mattie's fight. Mattie seemed more even tempered and had even begun preparing for the student art show at the end of the school term. She and Kate had decided not to say anything to Mattie about Angel drugging their drinks. They couldn't prove it, and neither of them wanted to know if Mattie either already knew and didn't care or didn't believe them.

"Happy birthday, September." Angel slipped an arm around Mattie's waist and took the drink from her. She took a swallow and handed it back. "Is it time to spank the birthday girl?"

September rolled her eyes in disgust. "I'm going back to the party. See you later, Mattie. I can't wait to see what you got me." September went back into the living room to find Kate. Angel's constant sex references made her skin crawl.

She saw Kate dancing with a girl from one of her dance classes and smiled. Kate looked terrific. She was wearing a short, tight blue velveteen dress that showed off her legs and made the blue of her eyes deepen to a sapphire color. Kate had great legs. She'd curled her hair and put on more than her usual lip gloss and mascara. September enjoyed being able to watch Kate for a few moments. Kate saw her and motioned for her to join them on the dance floor.

After several songs, Kate stopped dancing and headed for the kitchen. "I've got to get a drink. You want another one?" September followed her.

"Yeah." September took the rum and Coke Kate fixed for her. "Nobody's touched the cake."

"I think they're waiting for you. Why don't we go find Mattie and you can blow out your candles and open your presents?"

"You didn't get those trick candles, did you?"

"Maybe." Kate laughed and ducked as September playfully swatted at her. They went back into the living room and began winding their way through the dancers, looking for Mattie. They kept getting stopped by friends giving September birthday wishes, or asking her or Kate a question, or making party small talk. They finally made their way to the front porch where a small group was smoking and expounding drunkenly on the meaning of life. Mattie and Angel weren't with them. Kate and September wound their way back through the living room, and into the hallway. September peeked into Mattie's studio, but it was empty. She heard voices coming from Mattie's room.

The sight of Mattie leaning over the lines of white powder on her desk with a small straw up her nose surprised September so much, she froze in the doorway and Kate bumped into her. September watched silently as Mattie finished snorting two lines of cocaine. She wiped her nose with the back of her hand, sniffed, and handed the small mirror they were arranged on to Angel, who was lying on the bed with her shirt unbuttoned.

Kate stood in wordless shock, a hand on September's shoulder. The glass September was holding slipped from her hand and shattered on Mattie's hardwood floor. Angel and Mattie looked up, startled, at the sound. Mattie tried to cover the rolling papers, razor blade, and other drug paraphernalia on the dresser before standing up and coming towards September.

"You promised!" September shoved Kate out of her way and strode into her room. Kate followed.

September grabbed her suitcases out from under her bed and began throwing clothes into them at random. Kate took the clothes she threw into the suitcases and folded each piece before putting it back. "September, talk to me. What are you doing?"

"I can't stay here. She promised. She promised me, Kate!" September stopped pulling clothes out of drawers and dropped onto the bed. Kate sat down beside her and put an arm around her. Lizzie had promised her too. Every time Lizzie had promised, September had believed her and given her the benefit of the doubt. She had overlooked so many red flags and signs that things weren't right because she had trusted Lizzie. If she had just trusted her gut, Lizzie might still be alive.

"I know. You can come stay with me." Kate started to run her hand up and down September's back, but she stood up and started emptying drawers again.

The door opened and Mattie rushed into the room. When she saw the open suitcases, she grabbed September's arm and tried to make her put the clothes she was holding back in the drawer. "September, what are you doing?"

"I told you I'd leave if you didn't stop."

"I know. I just–it's hard. Don't leave me. I need you." Mattie's face crumpled and her eyes filled with tears. September felt her resolve start to soften but the image of Lizzie's broken body filled her mind and hardened it again.

September pulled her arm away from Mattie and kept packing. Kate kept folding the clothes she was throwing randomly in the suitcases, mostly to keep herself busy. She was worried about September. She seemed way too calm, and her face was a mask.

"I can't stay here, Mattie. I told you I would leave if you didn't stop." September dumped her armload of clothes into a suitcase. Mattie grabbed the clothes out of the suitcase and threw them on the floor.

"I won't let you leave! You have to stay. Give me one more chance! I swear I'll really do it this time."

September picked her clothes up off the floor and put them back in her suitcase. Mattie grabbed her arm and September jerked away.

"You don't get another chance. I can't do this anymore. I'm not going to watch you kill yourself. I'm moving in with Kate."

Mattie dumped another of her suitcases on the floor. September closed the other two and picked them up. Mattie reached out and grabbed the suitcases. She threw them back on the bed and roughly grabbed September by the shoulders. "You're not going anywhere. I don't want you to leave."

"Let go of me!" September pulled free of Mattie's grasp and went to pick up her suitcases. Mattie grabbed her arm, swung her around, and slapped her across the face. She shoved September to the ground before Kate was able to grab her and pull her away.

"September, please. Listen to me." All of the anger seemed to have suddenly drained out of Mattie. September stood up and picked up her suitcases. Kate could see she was shaking.

"Kate, let's go." She shoved past Angel, who had come to stand in the doorway, still with her shirt unbuttoned, watching the scene in September's room. "I'll get the rest of my things later."

Several of the guests had left when they heard Mattie yelling. The ones that remained were standing in silence near the edges of the room. The CD had stopped playing, but no one was moving to replace it. They watched as September headed towards the front door with Kate behind her. Mattie suddenly ran to the table, picked up the cake and hurled it towards them. It hit the door and left a long purple and white smear of frosting with hunks of chocolate cake clinging to the door as it crumbled onto the floor. September and Kate sidestepped the mess and left. As Mattie went into a rage and began pulling pictures off the walls, the guests who remained quickly gathered their things and left.

Chapter 28

September couldn't sleep. She opened the door to Kate's bedroom and slipped between the sheets into the bed beside her. Kate woke up when she felt September lay her head on her shoulder. Hoping September couldn't hear how fast her heart was beating, Kate slipped her arms around September. She stroked her hair and waited for her to speak.

"Thank you for letting me stay here. I can't go through that a second time. I just can't."

"A second time?"

September took a deep, shaky breath. "Summer before our junior year, Lizzie met this guy, Brent. He worked at the mall, and they met at the food court when she got a job at a store there."

"Lizzie? Your friend who—your friend from your old college?"

"Yeah. I wasn't crazy about him. I thought he drank too much and there were rumors about him being a drug dealer."

Kate wasn't sure what Lizzie had to do with September's moving out, but she had a feeling she was about to find out how Lizzie died. She waited silently for September to continue.

"She started smoking pot, I didn't know at the time, but she was doing other drugs too. She got fired from her job, she never wanted to do anything anymore. We were drifting apart." September's voice trembled and Kate felt a tear hit her shoulder.

"She convinced me to go to a party with her the last week of school. She pretty much ignored me the entire party before disappearing entirely. I decided I'd had enough and went looking for her to tell her I was leaving. I found her with him in a bedroom. She was completely wasted. She could barely walk. He told me to take her home with me." September swallowed and took another shaky deep breath. Kate felt September begin to shake and when she spoke again, her voice was thick with tears.

"I've never told this to anyone. I hit my head, so when I told everyone I didn't remember how the accident happened, they believed me. But I do." September was silent for so long, Kate thought maybe she had fallen asleep or decided not to continue.

"I managed to get her into the passenger seat, but I couldn't get her buckled in. I figured it didn't matter. We didn't have far to go. She was passed out when I started the car, but she came to on the way home. She thought I had forced her to leave. She was mad and she was yelling at me to turn around. I wouldn't do it, so she started hitting me and grabbed the wheel." September was sobbing by this time and could barely get the words out. Kate felt tears well in her own eyes as she held September tightly. When she spoke again, Kate could barely hear her.

"She–I couldn't control the car and we went off the road. The car–there was a ditch, and the car rolled over. We landed on a small tree growing out of the side of the ditch. We were–we were pointed straight down. I was–you saw my scar, but-but she–." September broke down and couldn't continue. September's guilt overwhelmed her. If she had just managed to get Lizzie's seat belt buckled, she wouldn't have been thrown from the car. Kate stroked her back for several minutes and murmured soothing noises in her ear. Kate felt the sobs begin to subside.

"They found ecstasy, speed and pot in her system. I was still in the hospital and couldn't go to her funeral." Kate felt September's hand move to wipe her eyes before she continued. "That's why I moved out here. I wanted to go somewhere I didn't know anybody, and I didn't have any memories." She paused and when she continued, her voice was shaky again.

"Mattie was so great at first. She made me laugh and helped me a lot. When she started–I didn't know about Lizzie and the drugs. I thought maybe I could save Mattie. She's my best friend and I didn't want to lose her so soon after Lizzie." September broke down and cried again. Kate hugged her, kissed her forehead, and continued stroking her hair as she let September cry.

Chapter 29

In the two weeks since September had moved in with Kate, she hadn't mentioned Lizzie and the accident again, so Kate didn't bring it up. It was obvious to her that September felt responsible for the accident even though she shouldn't. They had gotten the rest of September's things on a day they knew Mattie would be out of the house. September had paid her part of that month's rent to the landlord so Mattie couldn't spend it on drugs but also had some time to find a new roommate. September didn't want to go out, so Kate had settled on trying to teach September to swing dance as a distraction.

"The poor neighbors! I can't believe you're trying to teach me to swing dance at midnight." September laughed as Kate tried to twirl her around the tiny living room again.

"It's Friday night. They're probably not home." Kate tried to spin September around and their feet got tangled, toppling them both onto the couch. They laughed breathlessly and tried to untangle their arms. Kate had landed on top of September. Before she could get up, September reached up, pulled Kate towards her and kissed her. Kate slid down onto the couch to lie next to September and kissed her again. "That was nice. What was that for?"

September smiled shyly. "I just wanted to. It's okay, isn't it?"

Kate swallowed as her heartbeat quickened. It was exactly what she wanted, but she wasn't sure September wasn't experimenting. "Yeah, it's more than okay."

"Good." September kissed Kate again, this time parting her lips to let Kate's tongue dart across hers. They continued to kiss, Kate letting September make all the first moves, so she didn't push her too fast. They had been kissing on the couch for several minutes when someone pounded on the door. September ignored it and continued to kiss her, but Kate tried to pull away as the knocking continued.

"Let me get the door."

"No, don't answer it." September tried to pull Kate back down, but she slipped out of her grasp and went to the door.

"Can I help you?" Kate thought the blue-haired girl in the ripped jeans and Boys Suck t-shirt looked familiar, but she wasn't sure how. She also had no idea why this girl was on her doorstep at midnight. The girl stared at Kate blankly for a moment.

"I'm looking for that girl with the weird name? A day or a month or something like that?" The girl was shifting nervously from foot to foot and staring at the ground.

"You mean September?" At the mention of her name, September came to the door behind Kate to see who was looking for her.

"That's me. Who are you?"

The girl looked relieved. "This is the fourth apartment door I've knocked on. You've got to come with me. Mattie's totally freaking out. Some guy said her old roommate–." September and Kate didn't wait for the girl to finish her story. They grabbed their coats and hurried out the door, shoving the girl down the steps in front of them.

They could hear Mattie screaming and the crash of breaking glass before they got out of the car. September and Kate glanced at each other apprehensively before getting out of the car and walking up the cracked sidewalk to the open front door of the house. People were standing in small groups in the bare yard, watching the door as if they expected Mattie to come running out wielding a weapon at any moment. September felt them staring at her and Kate as if they were wondering how they were possibly going to put an end to what was going on inside the house.

There were still a few people inside the house's small living room. They were clutching their drinks and standing as far away from the hall as possible. The house smelled strongly of marijuana and some other substance September couldn't identify. The screaming briefly subsided, and September breathed a sigh of relief right before the sound of something large hitting the closed bathroom door reverberated throughout the small house. Kate jumped slightly beside September.

"Are you sure you want to talk to her?" Kate put a hand on September's shoulder.

"No. Wait out here for me." September stepped up to the door and knocked softly.

"Go away!"

"Mattie, it's me. It's September. Please talk to me." September placed a hand on the door. "Please."

All the sound from within the bathroom stopped. September stood by the door, holding her breath. Just when she was about to give up and have Kate call for an ambulance, the door opened a fraction of the way and Mattie's hand reached out. She grabbed September's arm and pulled her inside, shutting and locking the door behind her.

Mattie threw her arms around September and collapsed against her, sobbing. September absently stroked Mattie's dark curls as the condition of the bathroom sank in. Mattie had ripped the shower curtain off of its rod and then pulled the rod down. The mirror was shattered, pieces of glass strewn all along the vanity and the floor. The medicine cabinet was open, and all of its contents smashed and thrown around the small room. Except for the bathroom fixtures, not a single thing in the bathroom had escaped Mattie's wrath. Makeup was smashed into one large, multi-color lump at the bottom of the sink and the towels lay in a heap in the tub, soaked in what appeared to be shampoo and conditioner.

"Mattie, what happened?" Gingerly, September picked her way through the mess, and sat Mattie down on the closed toilet seat. She found a place along the edge of the tub and sat down beside her. Mattie was crying so hard; September was afraid she was going to start hyperventilating. Mattie was gasping for air, trying to calm down enough so she could talk. Finally, she was able to speak even though she was still crying.

"I've been trying really hard to stop using since you moved out." Mattie took a deep, shaky breath and continued. "Angel wasn't happy about it. Tonight, she wanted me to do some X with her and Ali. I told her no and she got mad." Judging by her bloodshot eyes and dilated pupils, Mattie had been using something earlier, but September kept quiet. Trying was good. "She left! She left with that fucking slut! I know they're off having sex right now. This isn't the first time she's done this. Now that I don't want to get high all the time and screw other girls with her, she doesn't want me."

Mattie dropped her head into her hands and started to cry again. September reached out and stroked Mattie's back and she struggled to get control. "I'm sorry, Mattie. I know you care about her." September struggled to find the right words. "Angel isn't–as long as you're with her, drugs are going to be a part of your life. I am so happy to hear that you're trying to get clean. I'm just not sure you can do that with Angel around."

"Of course I can! I can't let her leave me, I can't."

"Why not? There are a lot of people who care about you and would love to help you. Kate's outside waiting for us. She's worried about you, just like I am."

Mattie shook her head. "You don't understand! When you left with Kate, Angel was the only person I had left. If I lose her, I lose everybody."

"That's not true! I love you, you're my best friend. It kills me to see you like this. You still have me, and you still have Kate too."

"It doesn't feel like it. I feel so alone, so worthless. Sometimes I think I should just kill myself. No one would miss me."

"That's not true. I would miss you." September whispered, trying to fight back the feeling of panic that was rising in her chest.

"No, you wouldn't. You're better off without me around. Look at what I did to you the last time I saw you. You say you care about me, so

I hit you." Mattie was quiet for a moment. Then she whispered, "I just want to stop hurting. That's all I ever wanted."

"Drugs aren't the answer. Call your parents. Ask them to get you some help."

"My parents wouldn't understand. They can't help me. They don't understand anything I care about. They keep telling me I should give up photography. They wouldn't tell me that if they cared."

"I met your parents and I know they love you. They are very worried about you. I know they'd help you."

"No. I have to handle this on my own. Nobody understands. No one cares about me."

"That's not true. Kate and I wouldn't be here if we didn't care." September reached out and put her hand on Mattie's arm. Her fingers slid in something warm and sticky. She looked down at Mattie's arm and noticed the blood for the first time. She couldn't believe she hadn't noticed it before. It was smeared all over Mattie's clothes and her arms. It was on September's shirt where Mattie had hugged her. She pulled Mattie's arms out towards her, immediately relieved to see the cuts didn't seem to be deliberate.

"You're bleeding!" September couldn't find a towel that looked clean, so she grabbed a wad of toilet paper and pressed it to what appeared to be the worst cut. She noticed bruises encircling both of Mattie's wrists.

"What happened to you? Why do you have all these bruises?"

Mattie stared at the floor and pulled her hands out of September's grasp. "It's nothing. Sometimes Angel likes to play a little rough, that's all."

"It is something, Mattie! When are you going to realize she's not good for you? She feeds you drugs, cheats on you, leaves bruises on you, and drugs your friends! How much more does she have to do–?"

"What do you mean she drugs my friends?"

"How do you think Kate and I ended up in bed the night of Heather's party? Angel spiked our drinks with X."

"She wouldn't do that. Why would she drug you?"

"I don't know. But she did it, and if you think about it, you know she did." September put an arm around Mattie and helped her stand up. "Come on, that cut hasn't stopped bleeding. I think you need to go to the doctor."

Chapter 30

Since classes were canceled on Martin Luther King Jr Day, Kate and September had decided to drive up to Albuquerque and go shopping for the day. Neither of them had a Tuesday morning class so they could drive back that morning. Kate had told September she had one last place she wanted to go.

"Where are you taking me?" September looked over her shoulder uneasily at the hotel across the parking lot. Kate laughed.

"Not there. Come on, follow me." Kate got out of her red Beetle and headed toward a dirt trail at the edge of the parking lot. September quickly followed.

She walked down the railroad tie steps behind Kate and hesitated slightly before following Kate off the path. "Are you sure about this? Don't rattlesnakes live in the mountains?"

"Too much noise right around here. Don't worry." Kate pulled herself onto a boulder and helped September up beside her. September stopped watching for snakes and looked out at the view. The whole city of Albuquerque stretched out below them.

"It's beautiful." September pulled her jacket tighter around her. She still had trouble remembering how quickly the temperature dropped at night in New Mexico.

"We're just in time for the sunset."

Kate and September sat quietly and watched the sun go down over the city, the sky fading into deep oranges, pinks and purples. September turned her head and studied Kate in the dim light. Strands of blond hair were blowing across her face in the breeze. September's mouth suddenly went dry. Kate was beautiful. September wanted to brush the hair away from her face and kiss her. She looked away and cleared her throat.

"Thank you for bringing me here."

"I've never brought anyone here before. This is my truth spot." Kate's voice was barely above a whisper.

"Your what?" September wrapped her arms around her to try and stop her shivering. Her jacket wasn't heavy enough for sitting outdoors.

"There's just something about this place. Whenever I have something tough I need to work out, I come here. I can't lie to myself here." Kate turned and stared into September's eyes. "Or to anyone else."

September had trouble reading the look in Kate's eyes in the deepening twilight. "I'm trying not to lie to myself anymore. Trouble is, I'm so confused sometimes, I don't know what the truth is."

"What do you mean?" Kate scooted a little closer to September to try and keep warm.

"I think maybe you were right about Lizzie. We kissed hello and goodnight and we hugged and slept in the same bed sometimes. I think that maybe I was in love with her, I just didn't know it." September paused and looked at Kate to try and gauge her reaction to the jumbled mess of feelings she had just confessed to. Kate nodded and September struggled to continue with what she wanted to say.

"I remember when Spring discovered boys. To her, kissing was like candy is to three-year-olds. I never really understood that until now. These feelings are all new, and I don't just mean realizing that I like women. I finally understand what the big deal about kissing and touching is and why people actually want to have sex."

Kate smiled when September compared kissing to candy. "What's the confusing part?"

"Mattie." September paused. "And you."

"Me?" Kate's voice was soft. She put an arm around September when she shivered again. Kate's arm around her shoulders felt good, and she didn't want her to move it, but it was going to make the next part harder to say.

"Did you ever notice how much like Lizzie Mattie looks?" Kate nodded. "I'm having a hard time figuring out if I'm attracted to Mattie because she reminds me of Lizzie or because of who she is."

"So, you're attracted to Mattie?" Kate suddenly sounded sad. September leaned her head on Kate's shoulder briefly.

"Yes. I like you too, but I'm afraid to mess up our friendship." September was afraid Kate hadn't heard her. Finally, Kate spoke.

"I've been attracted to you for a long time. I didn't want to say anything because you weren't sure of yourself, and then–I know it might be weird since we're roommates, but–." Kate took a deep breath. "I brought you up here because I wanted to ask you out for Valentine's Day."

"Really? I'd like that." September smiled and bit her lip. She couldn't believe Kate wanted to go out with her. She hoped she didn't screw it up.

"You will?" Kate smiled. She caressed September's cheek, leaned in and kissed her.

September kissed her back before pulling away. "Did you hear that? Was that a snake?"

Kate laughed. "No, that was my keys, but we should probably go. Your nose is freezing." She helped September off the boulder before grabbing her hand to lead her back to the car.

Chapter 31

The anticipation had been killing Kate, especially since neither she nor September had brought up their feelings again since the mountains, but it was finally time for their date.

"These are for you." Kate handed September a dozen purple roses as she stepped into the house. September lifted them to her face and inhaled their scent. She smiled and gave Kate a one-armed hug.

"Thank you. They're beautiful. I can't believe you sent me flowers twice in one day." September carried them into the kitchen to put them in a vase. She put two of the roses into a separate bud vase and set it on the table she had set for their dinner before putting the vase with the rest of the roses next to the vase of daisies on the coffee table.

Kate had asked her on a real date. September was nervous about her first real date with a woman being with the woman she was living with, but she was attracted to Kate and knew Kate wouldn't push her faster than she wanted to go.

"Twice? I didn't get you any other flowers." Kate looked at the daisies. "What made you think I sent them?"

"The card said, 'See you tonight.' They were sitting in front of the door when I got home from the grocery store. I just assumed." September shrugged.

"The delivery guy probably made a mistake. Some poor guy is probably trying to explain to his girlfriend that he really did send her flowers and he can't understand why she didn't get them." Kate laughed. She looked at September and smiled gently. "Are you nervous?"

"A little. Usually, the people I go out with haven't seen me naked before our first date." September smiled. Kate looked beautiful in the red velvet dress she was wearing. "I'm glad it's you though."

September lit the candles on the table, and they sat down to the dinner she'd made. Neither of them ate much, they were both nervous, but the conversation flowed as smoothly as always.

"That was delicious. Thanks for making dinner. We could have gone out, so you didn't have to cook."

"I like to cook. It relaxes me. It was good for me to cook today." September motioned for Kate to sit on the couch. "I have something for you too. Let me go get it."

September went into the kitchen. Kate heard a cabinet door open. What had September gotten her? September approached Kate with her hands behind her back. Standing in front of Kate, she presented her with a necklace she had made and a box of chocolates from Godiva. "I remembered how much you like these."

"Thank you. It's beautiful." Kate fingered the necklace wrapped around the chocolate box. September had been inspired by the evening they'd watched the sunset together and had created a necklace for Kate in various shades of blues, pinks, and purples. Blue was her favorite color on Kate.

Godiva chocolates weren't available in Portales, so September had called Spring and asked her to overnight the gold box to her earlier that week. Spring had sent her a care package with another box for herself, a card, some candles, and a copy of the Better Than Chocolate movie. Included was a note to enjoy the evening and have as much fun as she wanted.

"Spring sent me a movie. Do you want to watch it?" September showed her the box.

"Sure." Kate moved over on the couch so September could join her. She settled back on the cushions and put an arm around September. To her secret pleasure, September leaned into her and put her head on Kate's shoulder. About thirty minutes into the movie, Kate reached for the chocolate. "I can't stand it anymore. I've got to have some of this."

September took the box from her. "Let me." She opened the box, selected a piece of chocolate, and fed it to Kate. Kate took the box and fed September a piece. Kate smiled.

"You've got some chocolate right there." Kate motioned to the corner of September's mouth. September smiled shyly and looked at Kate through half-closed eyes.

"Will you get it for me?" Kate leaned in and kissed September. She kissed Kate back, taking the chocolates from her and setting them back on the coffee table. September put her arms around Kate's shoulders. She nibbled lightly on Kate's bottom lip, making Kate groan with pleasure. Kate leaned back, pulling September on top of her.

Kate was running her thumb along the edge of her bra, making September very aware of Kate's hand on her rib cage. The feel of Kate's hand right underneath where she wanted it was driving September crazy. She loved kissing Kate, but she wanted more. She wanted Kate to move her hand up, onto her breast. September slid her hand down Kate's arm, onto her hand, and pushed Kate's hand onto her breast, arching into her at the touch.

Kate gently bit September's neck one more time and whispered in her ear. "Are you sure this is okay?"

"Yes." September moaned as Kate gently pinched her hardened nipple in her fingers. September slid her hand up Kate's waist to her chest. It felt natural to touch Kate like she wanted Kate to touch her. "Can I–?"

"Please." Kate groaned as September rubbed her thumb across the velvet covering Kate's hardened nipple.

They had been kissing, making out, and ignoring the film for about twenty minutes when someone began knocking loudly on the door. September ignored the knocking until it became so loud, they couldn't ignore it anymore. September reluctantly pulled herself away from Kate and answered the door. Tony pushed past her into the living room. Kate looked at him in confusion and remained seated on the couch.

"September, I've got to talk to you."

"Tony, what are you doing here?" September stared at him in amazement as she reached up to see how badly her lipstick was smeared. She couldn't believe he was standing in her living room. She hadn't spoken to him since she'd broken up with him at Christmas. How did he know where she was living now? With sickening certainty, she knew who sent the daisies.

"Baby, I love you. I know we're supposed to be together." Tony reached out and clasped one of her hands in his. She pulled it away and backed away from him.

"Tony, I–"

"No, don't say anything, just listen to me. I know what you said about being confused and wanting to date other people. Baby, I've been thinking, and I think you're just confused because we aren't together while you're here."

September's knees weakened. She hadn't told Tony whom she wanted to date when she'd broken up with him. She sank into the armchair behind her. "Tony, don't. Please. I don't–."

"Baby, I know you. You don't really want to date someone else. You're just confused because we don't see each other all the time anymore and because of what happened to Lizzie. I'll transfer out here next semester and–."

"No! Don't transfer out here. I am not confused about my feelings for you. Don't you remember Christmas? We aren't dating anymore." Kate remained frozen on the couch, not sure whether to interrupt or let them talk. She knew September hadn't said anything to Tony about wanting to date women.

"If I was out here all the time–." Tony grabbed her hand and knelt down by her.

"Tony, it wouldn't help."

"I love you, September." Tony held onto her hand as she tried to take it back.

"You don't love me, Tony. You don't even know me anymore. Why are you doing this?" September put her head in her hands and let her hair fall over her face to hide herself from Tony's gaze.

"Of course, I know you. We've been going out for–."

"No. We were going out. We're not a couple anymore. You can't possibly know me because I don't know myself half the time." September stood up and pulled out of Tony's grasp. She walked away from him towards Kate.

Stunned, Tony looked around for the first time. He saw his flowers next to the ones Kate had given her. He saw the remnants of the romantic dinner September had made and all the flickering candles supplying the soft glow of light in the room. "If we just spend more time together. I'll transfer, and we –."

"Tony, I said no!" September closed her eyes and took a deep breath to calm herself. She hadn't wanted to do this, but she didn't see that she had much of a choice. "Spending more time with you isn't going to help." September positioned herself between Tony and Kate, unsure of his reaction. "This is Kate. She's my date. She's the one I was talking about at Christmas."

Tony stared at the petite blond sitting on the couch. Kate smiled uneasily and stood up, not sure what she should do or say. He shook his head in disbelief. "A girl? You dumped me for a girl? I don't understand."

"I don't understand it completely myself, Tony. I'm sorry. I didn't know how to tell you. Since I came out here, I've been attracted to women. This is something I have to explore. I didn't mean to hurt you."

Kate picked up her coat from the back of the armchair and headed towards the door. "You two should talk. I'm going to go grab some coffee. I'll be home later."

"No, Kate, don't leave. Please." September put a hand on her arm to try to stop her. Tony stood up.

"You live with her? God, September, how long has this been going on?" Tony stood staring at her for a moment. September flinched at the pain in his eyes. She'd never wanted to hurt him. He was a good guy. He just wasn't the right guy for her. "I'm the one who should leave. Clearly, I was mistaken. I didn't mean to bother you. Forget I came here." Tony left and a moment later they heard his car roaring out of the driveway.

"It's getting kind of late. I really should go to bed. I've got an early rehearsal tomorrow. We'll talk later, okay?" Kate awkwardly kissed September's cheek and hurried to her room. September sighed, locked the front door behind Tony and sank back down into the armchair.

What a disaster. Kate is never going to want to go out with me again. Why did Tony have to show up tonight of all nights? What was Tony thinking? The thought of him transferring to Portales made her shudder. The memory of Kate's touch crept into her head and the shudder that went through her this time brought a smile to her face. She had to get Kate to give her a second chance.

Chapter 32

September struggled to keep hold of her backpack and the groceries she was carrying as she fought to unlock the door to her and Kate's apartment. She dropped her backpack onto the floor right inside the front door. She froze when she saw the attractive, dark-haired girl sitting on the couch.

The girl smiled, stood up, and took one of the bags from her. "Hi. You must be September. It's nice to meet you. I'm Piper. Kate's told me all about you."

"Hi." September eyed Piper warily. She didn't know who this girl was. Kate had never mentioned the brunette helping her carry the groceries into the kitchen. September pulled a box of cereal out of one of the bags and put it in the cabinet. "Is Kate here?"

"She's getting ready. She'll be out in a minute."

September watched as Piper put the milk and soda in the refrigerator. Who did this girl think she was? She was acting like this was her home. What did she mean Kate was getting ready? Getting ready for what? Based on the way Piper was dressed, it wasn't a dance rehearsal. Oh God, was Kate going on a date? Neither of them had talked about the disastrous way their date had ended two weeks earlier. September wasn't sure how to bring it up and she had been afraid Kate would say no to a second chance. She sighed. Kate must be moving on.

"What are you doing in here?" Kate was startled when she saw September in the kitchen with Piper. "September. I—I didn't think you'd be home so soon."

"Class was canceled." September studied Kate closely. Kate was wearing a dress and she had on lipstick. Her eyes locked on Kate's neck. She was wearing the necklace September had made for her. Kate must have felt September's gaze on her neck, because she reached up and covered the necklace with one hand.

"Our reservations are for six. We should probably go." Piper set the bag of tomatoes she was holding on the counter.

"Reservations?" September held Kate's gaze.

"Kate finally said yes to a date. We're going to dinner in Clovis and then to a movie." Piper smiled at Kate. She linked her arm through Kate's and led her towards the front door. September watched her go with a sinking feeling in her stomach.

She needed to cook. She needed to cook something time-consuming and complicated that involved lots of chopping. Indian would be good. September twisted her hair up out of her face, secured it with a claw clip, and put on an apron. She pulled out her well-worn cookbook and found the recipes she wanted. Alternately slamming cabinet doors and leaving them open, she pulled out all of the ingredients and utensils she needed.

The vegetable samosas and basmati rice were done, and she was just beginning the stir-fried kale with ginger when the phone rang.

"Hello?"

"What's wrong?" Spring always seemed to know.

"Nothing's wrong." If she didn't say it, she could pretend it wasn't true.

"Then why are you pulverizing whatever you're chopping? I can hear how hard you're beating that poor vegetable from here." Spring was trying to hide the amusement in her voice.

"I am not pulveri–!" September stopped mid-sentence and put down her knife when she realized the kale was nothing but pulp. She sighed. "I don't know what's wrong."

"What are you cooking?"

"Indian food." September's choice of what to cook told those who knew her a lot about her emotional state.

"Wow. Talk to me. Maybe we can work it out together."

"I don't know what's wrong. I was in a good mood. I have more time to study for that big test because class was canceled. I got home and this-this girl was here and–."

"What girl?"

"Piper." September spit the name out. "She's probably all of eighteen. She started putting away groceries like she lived here! She was all over Kate like she owned her, just because Kate agreed to go on a date with her." The sinking feeling was back.

"September, you're jealous." Spring lost her battle not to laugh.

"No, I'm not! Why would I be jealous?" September's protests sounded lame even to her own ears.

"Because you like Kate and she's out with someone else." Spring's voice was gentle. "Sweetie, it's okay to be jealous. You like her. Have you told her?"

"It wouldn't matter. After Tony's scene on Valentine's Day, she doesn't want to go out with me again."

"Did she say that?"

"She didn't have to. She's out with someone else and she didn't tell me about it first." September threw the pulverized kale in the trash. Now that she was talking to Spring and admitting what was bothering her, she didn't need to cook. She began cleaning up the kitchen. She wasn't hungry anymore and the rice and samosas would keep.

"Do both of yourselves a favor and talk to her."

"She was wearing the necklace I made her." September's eyes welled with tears. "She's out with someone else wearing my necklace."

"I'm so sorry. I know that's got to hurt. You need to talk to her."

"I will." September sniffed. "I just need–." September heard Kate's key in the door. "She's home. I'll call you tomorrow."

September hung up without waiting for an answer. She wiped at her face to make sure there were no tears. September walked into the living room hesitantly, afraid she might walk in on something she didn't want to see. Kate was alone. She smiled awkwardly at September.

"Hi. It smells good in here."

"I cooked. It's in the fridge if you're hungry." September stared at Kate, unsure what she should say or do. Kate sat down on the couch and patted the seat beside her. September sat down and began twisting a strand of hair that had escaped from her clip.

"I should've told you about my date with Piper. I'm sorry. She was a–test that didn't go like I thought it would." Kate paused. "She won't be back."

"What kind of test?"

"It's not important." Kate sighed. "Tony showing up really freaked me out. I thought you'd broken up with him, and he showed up wanting to transfer here."

"I did break up with him! I don't know why he showed up. I haven't talked to him since then, except for–."

Kate smiled sadly and put a hand on September's shoulder. "I know. But he didn't know why you broke up with him because you didn't tell him that." Kate brushed the strand of hair out of September's face.

"Kate, I–." The gentle pressure of Kate's finger pressed against her lips stopped her. Her lips burned to feel her touch again when Kate took her finger away.

"I like you. I really do." September opened her mouth to say something, but Kate shook her head. "You still haven't fully accepted that you were in love with Lizzie. I know you have feelings for me, but until you sort out whether you have feelings for Mattie, or if she just reminds you of Lizzie, I don't think you should be with anyone. You need to know what you want first."

September closed her eyes and took a deep breath. Kate was probably right. She didn't want to admit it though. Kate stood up and kissed September's forehead. The spot where Kate's lips had been felt cold at the loss of her touch.

"I like you, but I don't want to be your experiment or your trial run. We can talk again when you know what you want."

Chapter 33

"So?" Spring handed her younger sister a Diet Pepsi and sat down on her bed beside her. September had gone home for spring break to hang out with her sister and help with some wedding planning. Kate hadn't wanted to go home, so she had invited her to go with her.

"What?" September looked at Spring, puzzled. She had no idea what Spring was talking about.

"So how are things going with Kate? I've been dying to know since you two got here, but this is the first time we've been alone."

September took a drink and sighed. "They're not. We're friends and roommates and that's it." September sounded like she was quoting someone. Spring frowned.

"I thought you were going to talk to her." Spring got up and started looking through the dresses in her closet.

"I did. Well, I tried to. She talked and I listened. She doesn't want to date me." September sighed. "She thinks I don't know what I want, and she doesn't want to get hurt. She said it's best if we're friends and roommates and that's it." September took another drink. The thought of just being friends with Kate made her miserable. "She's probably right."

"Please, I've seen her when she thinks no one's looking. That girl wants you."

"Really?" September couldn't help the note of hope that crept into her voice. She sighed. "It won't matter. Kate's made up her mind." September set her soda can on Spring's nightstand and joined her in front of the closet. "Not that one." She took the green dress out of Spring's hand and hung it back up in the closet.

"First of all, you do know what you want, you just don't want to admit it." Spring took out a black dress and held it up to her. She shook her head and put it back. "Secondly, I think if you take Kate to the party tonight and let me dress you up, she won't be able to resist you. If you want her, you have to go after her."

"I don't know. I don't really want to go to the party." September pulled out a blue empire waisted dress out of the closet and held it out to Spring. "This one."

"I forgot I had this one!" Spring held it up to her, looked in the mirror, and smiled. "You have to come! You always come to the suave party. It's at Mark's parents' house this year. They live in Nichols Hills. They have an indoor heated pool and three hot tubs. When Kate sees you in the bikini I'm going to loan you, she won't be able to say no."

"Tony will be there, and I don't want to see him."

"It's a big house, you probably won't even run into him. He'll probably have his girlfriend with him anyway." Spring pulled out a deep purple dress and handed it to September.

"He's dating someone?" September was shocked.

Spring stopped primping in front of the mirror and turned to look at her younger sister. "Does that bother you?"

"No." September shrugged. She was genuinely happy for him. "I'm just surprised. He wanted to transfer schools for me a month ago, and now he's–I just didn't think he would be dating so soon. I'm glad he has a girlfriend."

"Come on, come to the party? Please?"

"Party?" Spring and September jumped when Kate entered the bedroom. Her hair was still damp from her shower.

"Mark's fraternity has a suave party every year. I'm trying to convince September that you two should come."

"What's a suave party?"

"It's an invitation only party where everyone dresses up in their suavest clothes. The fraternity has a wine bar and hors d'oeuvres and it starts off as this formal event but morphs into the usual debauchery by the end of the night."

Kate smiled. "Sounds like fun. Why don't you want to go?"

"Tony belongs to Mark's frat. I didn't want to see him, but Spring says he's got a girlfriend now. Do you want to go?" September doubted Kate was going to want to see Tony again. Spring stood beside her, nodding her head yes enthusiastically.

"I didn't bring anything to wear."

Spring pulled a short, black cocktail dress out of her closet. "This would look great on you."

Kate looked at September. "Are you cool with going?"

September hesitated briefly before nodding. If Tony was dating someone else, he ought to be fine with them being there.

"Yay!" Spring clapped her hands and pulled another dress out of her closet for September. "Bring a bathing suit and pack an overnight bag just in case. Mark said we can spend the night if we need to. We need to go in about an hour. I told Mark I'd be there early to help set up."

The drive from Norman to Nichols Hills passed quickly, all three girls talking, laughing, and singing along to the radio. They helped set up for the party and before they knew it the party was in full swing. September was glad they had convinced her to come. She loved the suave party, and this year was no exception. She was looking forward to the hot tub later. The drive had made her shoulder hurt and she was hoping the heat would help.

"Have you changed yet?" Kate knocked on the bathroom door. "Hurry before someone else finds the hidden hot tub."

"I'm almost ready. Why don't you go ahead and go down? Get us some drinks and I'll be right there." September looked in the mirror again. She tugged on the top of the bikini her sister had loaned her. The top barely covered anything. She sighed. At least the bottom wasn't a thong. She couldn't go downstairs like this. Where was that sarong Spring said she was going to put in the bag? September dug around and found the sheer black cloth. She tied it around her hips and looked at her reflection. She still felt way underdressed, and her scar was showing, but Kate was waiting. This was going to have to do. She pulled her hair forwards to cover her shoulder and headed to meet Kate.

As soon as September hit the stairs the cheers and cat calls started. September forced herself to look straight ahead and keep walking. She stopped and blinked. At the bottom of the stairs, Tony had Kate by the arm and was having a heated discussion with her. September rushed down the rest of the stairs to where they were standing.

"Tony, what are you doing? Let her go." September tried to free Kate's arm from his grasp. Tony turned to look at her, eyes blazing.

"She doesn't belong here. Neither do you. I can't believe you had the nerve to show up uninvited with your girlfriend at my frat's–!"

"She's not my girlfriend!" September hissed, looking around to see if anyone had heard Tony.

"When I came to see you, your lipstick was smeared all over her face. What would you call her?"

"She's my roommate. Tony–."

"Fine. It's time for you and your roommate, or whatever she is, to go." Tony took both of them by the arm and tried to escort them to the front door. He stopped when Mark and Spring stepped in front of the door.

"Tony, is there a problem?"

"No, Mark. I was just escorting these two party crashers out."

"September and Kate are my guests. Please let go of them and let them get back to the party."

"They don't belong here! My ex-girlfriend and the girl she cheated on me with don't belong at–."

"I never cheated on you! There is nothing going on with me and Kate!"

Mark looked at Spring. He looked at everyone who had gathered around to watch the scene. "Brad, turn that music back up. This is a party!" He looked Tony in the eye. "Why don't we all go upstairs and discuss this privately?" They followed Mark to a room upstairs. "Now, what is this all about?"

"I don't want them here. She cheated on me, lied about it, and brought her new lover to our party! She knew I would be here." Tony stopped and turned on September. "Look at you! I used to beg you to dress a little sexier. I bought you a bikini like that and you refused to wear it! Why for her? What's she got that I don't have?"

"It's March. I wasn't planning on coming to the party. I borrowed this from Spring. I never cheated on you, I never lied to you. I broke up with you before I went out with anyone else. The only reason I came to this party was because I was told you have a girlfriend and I thought you'd be okay."

"You never lied to me? You're still lying to me! You keep saying she's not your girlfriend, but I saw you two on Valentine's Day! You told me–."

"One date. We went on one date that you interrupted! She's my friend and she's my roommate. That's all she is. We made a mistake and went out once. It was way after you and I broke up."

Kate stared at September for a moment. Her blue eyes turned stony. She turned and walked towards the door. September turned to watch her. "Kate, where are you going?"

"I'm not in the mood for a party anymore. I'm going to change my clothes and then I'd like to go home."

September was stunned for a moment. Kate was obviously upset with her, but she wasn't sure why. "Okay. Spring, will you–?"

"I'm going to stay here with Mark tonight. Take my car. Mark will bring me home tomorrow."

The thirty-minute drive from the party to Spring's apartment in Norman was silent, except for the radio. They pulled up to the apartment building and Kate finally spoke.

"What are we doing here?"

"Spring's staying at Mark's. We need to talk, and I think it's best if we do it where we can be alone."

"I'm tired. I don't want to talk; I just want to go to bed." Kate tried to head down the hall, but September blocked her way.

"You're not going to bed until you tell me why you're angry with me."

"If you think going on a date with me was such a big mistake, why did you get so upset when I went out with Piper? If you didn't want to go out with me, you should've just said so."

"What? I don't think our date was a mistake." September's stomach clenched. She hadn't thought Kate would take what she'd said to Tony so seriously. "I just–there were so many people around, and I wasn't–."

"How can I be sure about that? You told Tony you never cheated on him, but that's not true. You were still dating him when you kissed Mattie and when you slept with me."

"That's not fair! Truth or Dare didn't count." September's eyes filled with tears of frustration. Truth or Dare did count. She knew it did, but she hated that she hadn't realized it at the time. If it had just been a nothing kiss for a stupid game, she would have told Tony about it, and he wouldn't have cared. She didn't tell him because it did mean something. "You know Angel–."

"I know. You're right about Angel, but the Truth or Dare kiss counted as cheating to me." Kate sighed. "I can't take it anymore, September. It seems like every time you take one step forward and I think you're finally going to admit who you are, you take two steps back, and I end up confused as to where I stand with you."

September stared at Kate. Panic seized her. She couldn't let Kate walk away angry. She had to convince Kate that she was worth it. The air between them was charged with tension. Slowly, September backed Kate against the wall and kissed her. Kate clung to September's shoulders and whimpered as their tongues slowly danced. September ended the kiss slowly with one last caress of Kate's tongue and press of her lips to Kate's. "And who, exactly, am I?"

"You're the woman who would break my heart if I let you. That's why we can only be friends until you make up your mind once and for all and can admit what you want." Kate slipped past September, walked down the hall, and closed the bedroom door behind her.

"Shit." September sank down on the couch. She'd blown it with Kate again, and Kate was right. She may not have meant to, but she had cheated on Tony. She knew she shouldn't have gone to the party. She got up and headed towards the bathroom. The sooner she went to bed, the sooner this night would be over.

Chapter 34

September groaned as she glanced at the digital clock on her bedside table. The glowing numbers read one o'clock in the morning. Who was that pounding on the door? She heard Kate get up to answer the door and threw an arm over her ear in an attempt to block out the noise. It had been four months since she had talked Mattie out of the bathroom at the party. Mattie was still dating Angel, but she didn't seem to be doing any drugs besides weed which was a big improvement. September was finally beginning to be able to sleep again without nightmares of Mattie following through on her threat to kill herself.

"September?" Kate knocked softly on her bedroom door, opening it just enough to stick her head into the room. "Are you up?"

"Go 'way." September mumbled, rolling away from the light spilling into her room from the hall.

"Mattie's here. I think you'd better get up." Kate's tone made September sit up, immediately wide awake. As she switched on the lamp beside her bed, the door opened all the way and Mattie limped in.

September stared at her in disbelief. Mattie's right eye was purple and rapidly swelling shut. The bruising continued down her cheek to her jaw. Blood was smeared across the bottom half of her face from a gash in her lower lip. Old and new bruises were visible all along her arms as Mattie gingerly removed the denim jacket she had on over her gray shirt.

September pulled her eyes away from the bruises on Mattie's arms. "I can't take this anymore, Mattie. If you're not here to tell me you're going to stop using for real this time and leave Angel, I don't want to see you."

"September, how can you–!" Kate's eyes widened in shock.

"I mean it, Kate! She has no idea what it's been like for us. I'm tired of sleeping with the ringer on the phone turned off because I'm afraid of it ringing in the middle of the night. I don't like being scared out of my mind every time the phone rings, because I think, this time, it's someone calling to tell me she's dead. I'm tired of pretending I'm not waiting for that phone call. I'm not doing it anymore. I can't." Tears shone in September's eyes as she struggled not to cry.

Mattie winced as she took the ice pack Kate offered her and gently applied it to her face. "I didn't know. I'm sorry." Mattie sat down on the bed, not able to stand on her ankle any longer. September moved over and wordlessly propped Mattie's ankle up on a pillow. "You were right about Angel."

"How?"

"I've been mostly clean since the party. Being so out of it I didn't realize I'd hurt myself scared me. Angel and I had a fight because I wouldn't give her money for drugs. I asked her if she drugged you two. She said no, and when I said I didn't believe her, she went nuts and started hitting me. I grabbed my keys and left."

"What made this time different?" Kate brought another ice pack for Mattie's ankle. She had her robe hanging open over her tie-dyed nightshirt.

"It was the first time I didn't think I deserved it." Mattie whispered, staring at her lap. She bit her lip and winced at the fresh burst of pain that brought on.

"Do you need a place to spend the night?" September hoped she wouldn't regret letting Mattie back into her house. She sounded sincere, but Mattie had made promises before.

"You're welcome to stay here." Kate yawned. "If you're okay, I'm going back to bed. I have an early class." Kate was about to close the door and go back to her own bed, when someone else started knocking on the door. Kate groaned. "Damn it! This is not Grand Central Station!" Kate went to see who was at the door this time.

"Mattie! Mattie, I know you're here!" Angel's voice floated into the bedroom. September stood up and hurried into the living room, shutting her bedroom door behind her. Angel was not getting her hands on Mattie again. She was surprised at Angel's appearance. It was the first time she'd ever seen Angel looking less than perfect.

Angel's mascara and eye makeup was smeared around her eyes, like she'd been crying. Her shirt was ripped, and her short blond hair was standing up on end. September and Kate could smell the alcohol on her.

"What are you doing here?" September's voice was cold. "How dare you come to my house looking for her after you–." Kate stepped in between September and Angel, put her hands on September's shoulders, and eased her towards the couch.

"It's okay, September. I should talk to her." Mattie stood in the doorway to the living room, holding an ice pack to her face, and the ice pack for her ankle in her other hand. Angel rushed to Mattie's side, running her hands over Mattie's hair and touching her black eye.

"I'm so sorry, baby! I didn't mean to do this. I was just so angry, I–."

Mattie shrugged Angel's hands off of her. "Do you mind if we talk in your room for a few minutes, September?"

"Mattie, I don't think–." September stood up, eyeing Angel apprehensively. She didn't think Mattie and Angel talking alone together was a good idea. She didn't want Angel in her house. She knew Mattie did need to end the relationship and she would rather have her do it where she and Kate could intervene if necessary.

"I meant what I said earlier. Don't worry." Mattie and September stared at each other for a moment. Finally, September nodded. Mattie took Angel into September's bedroom and shut the door behind them.

"I don't like this, Kate."

"All we can do is trust her that she means it this time." Kate yawned. She grabbed September's hands and pulled her up off the couch. "Come on, you can sleep in my room."

September rubbed a hand over her eyes and pushed her hair out of her face. Trying not to glance at the clock, she stumbled out of Kate's bedroom into the hall. She wasn't sure what had woken her up but as long as she was up, she might as well go to the bathroom. She noticed the door to her room was still closed and the light was on. She had fallen asleep waiting to hear the front door close when Angel left. *If she let that bitch sleep in my bed, I'll kill her*, September thought.

The bathroom door opened part way, and then bumped into something. September pushed against it harder and opened it a little wider. She squeezed through the door and froze. Mattie was sprawled on her back on the floor, arms flung out to her sides, hair covering half her face. "Mattie?"

September dropped to her knees and shook Mattie but got no response. "Kate! Kate, call 911!" September yelled. Kate ran into the bathroom, cordless phone in hand.

"Eight-twenty Avenue M, apartment number three. I don't know. My roommate–oh my God! Our friend passed out!"

"I need you to check if she's breathing and start CPR if she's not. Do you know how to do that?"

"Yes." Kate handed September the phone and started CPR on Mattie.

"Is this the roommate? Do you know what happened?" The man on the other end of the phone's voice was calm.

"I think she overdosed."

"On what?"

"I don't know. I'll look." September set the phone down beside Kate and went into the bedroom. Angel was asleep on her bed in her bra and jeans. September glanced around the room. When she didn't see any drugs, she shook Angel. Angel moaned and tried to shove September away. "Wake up, Angel!"

When September wouldn't quit shaking her, Angel finally opened her eyes. "What?"

"What did you give her?" September slapped Angel when she started to close her eyes again, not answering. "What did you give her?"

"I didn't give her anything." Angel wouldn't look at September.

"You're lying! She's unconscious on the bathroom floor! What did you give her?" September grabbed Angel's purse and started pulling things out and throwing them on the bed, searching for anything that looked like drugs. Angel tried to stop her. In the bottom of the bag was a plastic baggie holding an assortment of pills.

September stared at it for a moment. She had no idea what any of the rainbow assortment of pills were, or how to tell which of them Mattie had taken. September shoved the bag under Angel's nose. "Which of these did she take?"

Angel shrugged. "I don't know."

"Well, think!" September grabbed Angel by the arm, dragging her off the bed and into the bathroom. "Pick up that phone and tell the operator everything in that bag!"

Kate was still performing CPR on Mattie with no response. Ambulance sirens suddenly cut through the air. September ran to the door and stood in the doorway, waving to the paramedics as they got out of the ambulance and hurried up the stairwell with a stretcher. "She's in the bathroom!"

September leaned against the hallway wall facing the bathroom and sank to the carpet. As she stared into the bathroom watching the paramedics work on reviving Mattie, her vision got hazy and everything around her faded away.

September tried to steer them back onto the road, over corrected, and then back again. September tried not to panic as she realized they had reached the stretch of the two-lane road that was surrounded on both sides by a deep ravine-like ditch filled with debris and trees defying gravity and growing out of the side of the ravine. They hit a big pothole right as Lizzie grabbed the wheel again, jerking it hard.

"Take me back!"

The wheels spun on the soft shoulder and September realized they had gone too far over to the side. The car was going over the edge. "Lizzie! Hold on!"

September saw the bottom of the ravine rushing towards them incredibly fast and at the same time in excruciatingly slow motion. Her stomach flipped with the car; her head smacked the side of the door. Things were happening so fast, September couldn't register everything at once and by the time she processed that they were upside down, they had flipped right back up again. Lizzie was thrown around the car. The seatbelt jerked her against the seat, accompanied with a loud bang and followed by blessed stillness, as September registered they had come to a stop as blackness crept into the edges of her vision and everything went black.

September jerked awake. She had no idea how long she had been out. Her head was pounding. The seatbelt was painfully tight, September wasn't sure if it was the seatbelt making it hard to breathe, or if she had broken a rib. She sat perfectly still, trying to breathe through the pain and calm herself down enough to comprehend their situation.

She realized at some point she had closed her eyes. September tried to take a deep breath, stopped when it hurt, and tried to isolate the pain into separate injuries. Her head hurt where she hit it on the car frame. Her face and chest hurt, her wrist hurt, but her shoulder hurt the most. There was a stabbing pain in her shoulder. Something warm and sticky was running down her arm. Count to three and open your eyes. She opened her eyes and immediately wished she hadn't.

With her eyes open, she could tell the car had landed nose down in the ravine. The air bag had gone off, partially obscuring the view of the ground through the where the windshield used to be. The car had landed on a small tree growing out of the side of the ravine. A limb had come through the windshield and had stabbed itself into September's shoulder.

Slowly, she turned her head. Lizzie wasn't in the seat next to her. Shit! She wasn't wearing her seatbelt! "Lizzie? Lizzie, are you okay?" With the movement, a wave of nausea and dizziness rushed over her. Trying not to move her head, September searched for Lizzie.

"No." September whispered. Lizzie was outside of the car, pinned between the hood and the ravine. She wasn't moving and September

couldn't see her face. September grabbed the tree limb with the hand she could move and tried to pull it out of her shoulder. She screamed as her hand slipped and she ended up falling farther onto the limb. She vaguely registered a siren and flashing lights before passing out again.

Kate abandoned her position in the bathroom beside Mattie as the paramedics took over and sat beside her. September snapped out of her memory and let go of her shoulder when she realized she was holding onto her scar. A police officer had arrived shortly after the ambulance, and he was interviewing Angel in the living room. Neither of them watched when the police took Angel out of the house in handcuffs. September reached over, took Kate's hand while tears rolled down her cheeks, and leaned her head on her shoulder as they silently watched the paramedics work to revive Mattie. Images of Lizzie covered in blood and stretched out on the road while the paramedics worked on her kept superimposing themselves over Mattie. When they wheeled the stretcher out of the bathroom, Kate stood up and went into her bedroom. She appeared a minute later in jeans and a flannel shirt.

"Are you coming to the hospital with me? I'll call Mattie's parents from there." Kate looked down at September, still sitting on the hallway floor. September shook her head. She couldn't face going to the hospital right now. Kate watched her for a moment, trying to decide whether to press the issue. She was worried about September. She seemed to be going into shock. She hadn't said anything since telling the paramedics where to go. "I'll call you when they know something, okay?"

September nodded. She kept seeing Lizzie on the bathroom floor, before the image changed back to Mattie. Kate hesitated for a moment, then bent down, kissed the top of September's head and gave her a brief hug. "She's going to be okay. It's not like Lizzie."

Chapter 35

Mattie had stayed in the hospital for a week and was finally being released. She had gotten a concussion when she hit her head on the bathroom floor and they had wanted her to detox completely. September finally seemed like herself again and Kate had finally stopped worrying.

Kate smiled as she watched September carefully packing the sculpture she had finally finished. "It's beautiful. Is that the one for Lizzie's parents?"

"Yes. I had to wait until Mike graded it, but now I can send it." September had finally broken through her creative block. Finding Mattie on the bathroom floor had released something inside and she had worked for three days straight before she finally collapsed in exhaustion and slept through a day and a half. She had not only finally fulfilled her promise to Lizzie's parents, but she had two pieces to send her mother for the gallery.

"What about the student art show? Mattie said the deadline was extended. Are you going to enter?"

"I picked up the forms yesterday." September glanced at the clock. Mattie was checking out of the hospital today and was supposed to come see them before she packed for rehab. "What time is she supposed to be here?"

September finished packing the sculpture. She straightened a picture on the wall that was already straight and moved on to fluffing the throw pillows on the couch. She smoothed her long black skirt and ran a hand over her hair to make sure none of it had fallen out of the clip. Kate grabbed September's hands and made her sit down on the couch.

"Soon. Relax, you're making me nervous." Kate sat down beside September and let go of her hands. September stood up and started pacing.

"I can't relax. What if she changes her mind about going?"

"She's our friend. It's going to be okay. Rehab is going to work, Angel's gone, she's going to be her old self again."

September sighed. She hoped Kate was right. When Kate had called from the hospital to say they'd pumped Mattie's stomach and she was going to be fine, her relief had quickly turned to anger. She had been so angry with Mattie for scaring her and breaking her promises for so long, she hadn't gone to see Mattie while she was in the hospital. Mattie had called her, but she hadn't answered. In her message, Mattie had told her she'd been doing a lot of thinking and she needed to talk to her when she got out of the hospital. September had no idea what Mattie wanted to say. She knew Mattie and Kate had been talking and had mended their friendship. The idea that Mattie and Kate might start dating again made September queasy.

The doorbell rang and Kate stood up as September nervously ran a hand over her hair again. "I'll get it." Kate opened the door and September stood motionless as Mattie stepped into the apartment.

She looked good. She'd put on a little bit of weight and her dark hair was shinier than before. Mattie's eyes were clear, the bruises were fading, and she wasn't as pale as September remembered her being. She was wearing jean cut-off shorts and a green camouflage t-shirt. As September watched Mattie hug Kate hello, all her remaining anger drained away, and she was left with nothing but immense joy to see Mattie alive and well. She stepped up behind Kate.

"It's my turn now." Kate let go of Mattie and stepped back. September put her arms around Mattie and buried her face in her hair. Mattie hugged her back tightly, holding on for several minutes. Finally, she let September go. Mattie wiped at the tears that had formed in her eyes.

"It's great to see you. I missed you." Mattie sat down on the couch.

"I missed you too." Kate and September sat down on the sofa with Mattie.

Mattie paused for a moment and then took a deep breath. "I want to thank you for everything you did for me. If you hadn't found me when you did and started CPR, the doctors at the hospital said I probably would have died."

"Mattie, let's not talk about that. You're fine now."

"I'm getting there. I will be fine."

Kate glanced at Mattie and stood up. "I've got to leave in about thirty minutes for a rehearsal. It's really good to have you back, Mattie. Good luck at rehab." Kate looked at September strangely before she went into her bedroom and shut the door. It almost looked like Kate was going to cry.

"You scared me." September couldn't hold it in anymore. "I thought you were going to die."

"I'm sorry. I can't imagine what that must have been like for you, after Lizzie." Mattie clasped her hands in her lap. "I'll apologize every day if you want me to." September shook her head.

"I'm just glad you're okay. You said you wanted to talk to me about something?"

Mattie cleared her throat. "Yeah. I had a lot of time to think while I was in the hospital. I talked to a counselor about why I started taking the drugs in the first place while I was making the decision to go to rehab. We talked about how rehab would help me look at how I can keep from repeating those patterns, and–."

"I recognize the idea. My therapist and I talked about it too." September smiled.

"Well, one of the things I realized is that I care about you."

"Well, I care about you too." September put her hand over Mattie's. "You're my best friend. You really helped me when I first got here."

Mattie shook her head. "That's not what I–." Mattie suddenly leaned in and kissed her. All of September's uncertainties about what she was feeling towards Mattie and Kate suddenly made sense. None of the sensations she'd had the first time Mattie had kissed her were happening. She surprised them both by pulling away.

"Don't."

"I don't understand. I thought you liked me." Mattie looked confused.

"I do. You're my best friend. It's just, too much has happened, you know?" September took Mattie's hand. She pushed her hair back as a strand fell across her cheek. "If you had kissed me like that after Gena's party, I–."

"It would've been different." Mattie's eyes were shiny with tears. "I'm sorry I'm too late."

September smiled at her shakily. "You were almost the right girl." She looked towards Kate's closed bedroom door. Kate was the one who'd been there for her all along. She wasn't confused anymore about who or what she wanted. Mattie hugged her and wiped at the tears on her cheeks. She smiled.

"Tell her. She loves you too." She stood up, "I've got a lot of packing to do. I'm going to go home." Mattie paused at the door. "I mean it. Tell her." September nodded.

September knocked softly on Kate's bedroom door before opening it and going inside. Kate was lying on her bed reading a book. "I thought you had rehearsal."

"I just said that. I thought you and Mattie needed some time alone. Did she leave already?" Kate put a marker in her book and set it aside.

"Yeah. She went home to pack." September sat down on the bed.

"Did she talk to you?" Kate's voice was soft.

"I told her she was too late." September reached over and took Kate's hand.

"What do you mean?" Kate involuntarily squeezed September's hand.

"You're the second person who's ever seen my tattoo." Kate looked puzzled but kept quiet so September could continue. "Do you remember what it looked like?" Kate nodded.

"They're forget-me-nots. They're symbols of hope and remembrance. I got it right before I moved out here. I didn't have any faith or hope in anything right after Lizzie died. Things were finally beginning to seem like maybe, just maybe they could be okay again. I got the tattoo in memory of her, but also to remind me to have hope." September squeezed Kate's hand.

"I had it put on my hip because I knew that way no one would see it unless I wanted them to. I wanted it to be seen only by people I love." September leaned in and kissed Kate softly. Kate slipped her hand around the back of September's neck and pulled her into a long, lingering kiss. When they broke apart, September whispered, "I'm sorry I didn't realize it sooner."

"It doesn't matter. You realized it, that's what's important." Kate pulled the claw clip from September's hair, tossed it to the side, and eased September back onto the bed. She ran her hands over September's face, delicately tracing the contours of her cheekbones, nose and lips with her fingertips. Gently, she kissed her way along September's hairline, along her jaw, to her mouth. September wrapped her arms around Kate and pulled her down to her, parting her lips to let Kate's tongue slide against hers. "I've wanted you for so long."

September released Kate and sat up. Wordlessly, she pulled her shirt over her head and reached behind her to unhook the lacy black bra she was wearing. The contrast between September's creamy pale skin and the black lace made Kate's mouth dry and increased the wetness between her legs. She reached out to help September slide the bra off her shoulders. Kate cupped September's breasts in her hands and September groaned, leaning forward to kiss her. September began to unbutton Kate's shirt. She stopped caressing September long enough to help her remove her own shirt and bra.

They lay back on the bed, stroking and kissing each other. Kate went slowly, wanting September's first time without any chemical enhancement to be special. They kissed and caressed their way down each other's bodies, taking pleasure in the silky texture and taste of each other's skin. September shivered in anticipation as Kate unzipped her skirt and slid it down her legs. By the time Kate finished kissing her way up and down September's body and began making her way towards the tangle of hair between September's thighs, she was more than ready. September gasped in pleasure as she felt Kate's mouth on her for the first time.

Being sober made sex with Kate even better than September remembered. The tingling sensation where Kate touched her wasn't as electric, but more sensual. September felt completely connected to her body and Kate's. She couldn't wait to give Kate the same pleasure she was receiving.

September lay in Kate's arms, lazily running her fingers up and down the back of Kate's hand. Kate kissed her hair. "I love you."

September kissed Kate's hand. "I love you too. Will you come to Spring's wedding with me next month? I want you to meet my family."

Kate laughed. "I've already met your family."

September rolled over to face Kate and kissed her gently. "I mean as my girlfriend."

"So, I sleep with you once and suddenly I'm your girlfriend, huh?" Kate tried to keep from smiling as she teased September but lost the battle.

"It was twice, and you'd better be. I have a very strict policy about who gets to take off my underwear." September gently tugged a piece of Kate's hair.

"Won't your parents be at graduation?"

"I'm not going to graduation so why should they? I have no desire to sit through an hour of boring speeches just to walk across a stage in a shapeless black robe and cardboard hat while my family sits so far away, they can't even tell which one is me."

"Let's not talk about graduation anymore. I don't want to think about it right now." Kate sighed. She still had one more year of school left.

"What do you want to think about?" September smiled as Kate's hand crept up her stomach to her breast and captured her nipple between two fingers.

"I don't want to think at all." Kate kissed her and rolled on top of September.

Mattie's Party Playlist

AKA My Inspiration Playlist

Two Little Girls Ani DiFranco
Bloodletting Concrete Blonde
#1 Crush Garbage
Sad Dress Belly
Enjoy the Silence Depeche Mode
Low Cracker
Not an Addict K's Choice
It's the End of the World as We Know It R.E.M.
Groove is in the Heart Deee-Lite
Seether Veruca Salt
Sex and Candy Marcy Playground
The Last Day of Our Acquaintance Sinead O'Connor
Trouble Me 10,000 Maniacs
Just Like Heaven The Cure
Down By the Water PJ Harvey
Pepper Butthole Surfers
Closer to Fine Indigo Girls
Doll Parts Hole
Head Like a Hole Nine Inch Nails
Undone-The Sweater Song Weezer
Criminal Fiona Apple
Loser Beck
Heart Shaped Box Nirvana
Fade Into You Mazzy Star

Acknowledgments

This book is a love letter of sorts to my college years. I actually attended Eastern New Mexico University and I look back on my time there fondly. Portales was a tiny town and there wasn't much to do, so house parties were common. Suave parties were indeed real, but they weren't held by the Greek houses and, like in Vegas, what happens at a suave party stays at a suave party. If we wanted to go out clubbing, we invited a bunch of people, piled into a couple of cars, and drove two hours to Lubbock, TX. The drive wasn't fun, but with the time difference we would leave the club at 2am and get home at 3am so we always got an extra hour of sleep!

Chris, RIP, I still think about you and miss you.

Diane and Rayna, without the two of you, I wouldn't have heard of Ani DiFranco, gone to Sisters and Brothers bookstore or Double Rainbow, or gotten up to half of the stuff we did. The two of you are forever in my heart.

Vivian, thank you for taking a chance on me. You were the best first a girl could hope for. I will, however, die on the hill that juice is meant to be drunk cold!

Laura, I will be forever grateful I ran into you at the Renaissance Fair that day. Some of my fondest memories involve sitting on your couch, eating homemade pizza and watching movies while you made jewelry. I learned so much about parenting and living from you.

To Brenda, who inspired Heather's outfit at the club. You wore it perfectly.

Much love and thanks to M.E. Carter and J.D. Hollyfield, not only for your books, but for your time, encouragement, advice, and willingness to share your knowledge with me. I appreciate it more than you know.

Thank you to my family. Wolf, we've been through a lot together and I can't imagine life without you. Thanks for putting up with my crazy and giving me the time and space to chase my dream. A special thanks to my kids for loaning me their names. Hopefully, they won't regret it.

Lastly, a big thank you to my readers. Thank you for taking a chance on my book, and hopefully for loving my characters as much as I do. If you enjoyed it, please consider leaving a review.

About the Author

I have always loved to write. I wrote my first book at thirteen years old. I like to think I've gotten better since then. I don't have any more dogs falling out of airplanes and now the right people falling love with each other, anyway. When I originally wrote this in 2000 as a thesis project, my advisor told me I would have to age my characters up or down, because nobody wanted to read about people in their 20s. After numerous rejections (indie publishing then wasn't what it is now), I concluded he was right, and set it aside. Turns out I was just about a decade ahead of the times! New adult is totally a thing now! Right?

I never quite gave up on the dream of being a writer, I kept at it but never did anything with it. Thanks to encouragement from some author friends, I decided to pull my manuscript out, dust it off, and here we are.

I live in Oklahoma with my partner and our four children, three dogs, a turtle, and several bugs (don't ask). By day I help keep Oklahoma's drinking water safe, by night I write books. In my spare time I like to knit, read, and watch baking shows.

www.ingramcontent.com/pod-product-compliance
Lightning Source LLC
Chambersburg PA
CBHW050511160726
48003CB00001B/254